Nothing Ventured

A NEW ENGLAND ROMANCE

AVERY SAMSON

Editor: My Brother's Editor

Cover Designer: Rachel Webb

Cover Photo: FXQuadro/Shutterstock.com

Dedicated to the girls from apartment 2.
Good surviving!

Nothing ventured, nothing gained.

GEOFFREY CHAUCER

Contents

CHAPTER
One

PUSHING open the door of her new campus apartment for the first time, Karlie could feel the rush of adulthood pouring into her. Okay, so maybe that was a little overdramatic, but at least they had managed to find something other than a dorm in the housing lottery. She couldn't believe their good luck in snagging the only apartment still available to them as incoming sophomores.

Wrestling with the first of several boxes, Karlie had made her way in the front door of the old Victorian house, managing not to fall over the stairs that were partially blocked by the door itself. Why would you build a house where the door only opens partway because of the stairs?

It was an old house that had been built in the 1800s for an upper-class family when the college was still new. The campus had bought it, along with several others, years ago to help ease the overcrowding on campus. It was an old orange-trimmed monstrosity that could only be described as atomic tangerine in color. It looked like a giant Creamsicle gone wrong.

Karlie was moving into the apartment two weeks before anyone else. Volleyball two-a-days started tomorrow, so she only had today to get everything moved from the storage unit she had rented for the summer.

Holding the keys in her mouth, she managed to haul the first load up the stairs to the second floor. She had agreed to share Room 2 with a friend from freshman year. Apparently, Room 2 was on the landing across from Room 1, not in the actual apartment. Setting the boxes down next to the door, she found the next key in the set to let herself in.

The room was strangely large for a bedroom. It also had a nonworking fireplace against one wall. Because every college student needs a focal point in their room? The floors looked original to the house, having never been restored, but at least it came furnished. There were two twin beds, two desks, and two tiny wardrobes for their clothes.

With a shrug, Karlie shoved the boxes into the room before grabbing her keys to explore the rest of the apartment. Unlocking the next door, she entered the main living area, taking in a horror show of a bathroom across from it. They had all been apprehensive about sharing a bathroom with seven women, but had assumed it would be large enough with several sinks and stalls.

Karlie stood with her mouth open, taking in the retrofitted broom closet. It had a tiny corner shower with a curtain that looked like it might have been hanging there through several decades of students. The sink was a tiny freestanding model with an equally tiny mirror over it. The only shelves were above the toilet and promised to fall off the wall with the addition of any weight.

Reaching slowly into the shower, Karlie flipped on the hot water. The trickle that eased out made her groan. The gym didn't have any air conditioning and it was August. Most of the colleges in this part of New England didn't spend the money to put in air conditioning.

But then they hadn't had to smell her after a three-hour practice in the summer. She had to have water pressure to get rid of that particular funk. Tonight's excitement would have to include a trip to the home improvement store for a new shower head.

Walking through the living room, she noted the couch and chair that had obviously been snagged from an episode of *Life After People*. The stains on both were unidentifiable but made for an interesting study in splatter patterns. With a shiver, Karlie made a promise to herself to never touch them without a towel or hazmat suit.

The kitchen wasn't much better, with a four-top table partially blocking the back door, an antiquated stove and a fridge still full of the summer tenants' food. Shoving the table over, she shimmied through the back door in hunt of the laundry room.

Climbing down the back steps that slanted strangely to the outside, she found what would come to be labeled the Buffalo Bill basement. Not after the guy who had an old western touring group of sharpshooters, but the guy who lowers the lotion down to you in a bucket.

The first part of the basement was scary enough, but that wasn't where the one washer and dryer were. No, they were around the corner in a second room that only required a cage door to be featured in an episode of *Criminal Minds*.

Karlie shot out of the basement in a hurry, mentally calculating if she had enough clothing to wait until someone else moved in to do laundry with her. At least they would know where she was last going when she disappeared mysteriously from that portal to hell.

Climbing back up the stairs, she noted the back door to the outside had a piece of plywood covering what used to be a window. It opened into the back parking lot that was permitted only for the offices in the house next door. She was now living in a house with a parking lot that she wasn't allowed to park in.

By that evening, Karlie had her stuff unboxed, had

emptied the fridge, installed a new shower head and liner and was ready to flop down in her beanbag to watch the television she had set up in her room on the mantel.

After a quick shower, she threw on a pair of sleep shorts and a tank top since she still didn't have any air conditioning. She had worked her way through a couple of episodes of *Supernatural* on Netflix when her stomach started to growl.

"So, do I walk through the creepy house to the kitchen? Do I creep through or stomp to let the crazy I'm sure is lurking in there know I'm coming?" With a sigh, she stood, grabbing her keys to go make some popcorn in the microwave. "Great, now I'm talking to myself." Picking up her phone, she decided to call her mom as she headed through the rest of the apartment.

"Hey, sweetie. How is the new place?" Karlie's mom couldn't come help move her in this year like she did her freshman year. They had driven from Texas all the way to New England in four days. Her parents had insisted she keep her truck since she would be living so far from home. They were also just cool like that.

"It's fine. I got everything moved in."

"Good. When does everyone else show up?"

"I think Gemma is supposed to move in some time on Wednesday for some honors thing."

"That's just a couple of days. Not too bad." Karlie listened to her mom tell her about what had happened at home since she left. When the microwave wound down from what sounded like a NASA launch, she grabbed the bag of popcorn out, dumping it into a large bowl.

Walking back through the apartment, she flopped down into her bean bag as she ended the call. It wasn't until they hung up that she realized she had locked her keys in the other part of the apartment. The door locked automatically and she didn't think twice about it while she was on the phone.

With a sigh, she picked her phone back up, punching in

the number for the university police. Since the housing office was already closed for the night, it was the only thing she could think of. She had to be in the gym early tomorrow and would be tied up all day. Besides, the bathroom was in there.

"University police," the voice on the phone said. Karlie had talked to the older woman who answered the phone on several occasions. It was the same person who answered when one of her friends had too much to drink last year and she needed help from EMS.

"Hi, my name is Karlie James. I've locked myself out of my campus apartment."

"I'll send someone over. Where are you, sweetie?" Karlie rattled off her information before walking down the stairs to wait for one of the university police officers.

She had met several of them last year and knew they were a nice group of both men and women. They were also always amazingly quick when there was a problem. This time was no exception, taking only about ten minutes for someone to arrive.

"Hi," Karlie said, wrestling the heavy front door open. It was pretty easy to see he was a police officer, since there were large windows in the front door. She wasn't expecting what stood on the other side of the door, however.

Assuming it would be one of the older officers, she stood with her mouth open, staring into the darkest brown eyes she had ever seen. He had to have been at least several inches taller than she was and was young. Really young for what was usually employed on campus. He had regulation short dark hair with a five o'clock shadow already showing on his face.

Looking down at his body, Karlie took in the short-sleeved uniform shirt he had obviously poured himself into earlier, hiding a Kevlar vest. She worried momentarily if the sleeves could even hold from ripping if he had to wrestle someone to the ground.

That idea made her eyes travel farther south to check out his uniform pants, complete with taser and gun attached. She found herself staring at his well-polished shoes when he spoke.

"Did I pass inspection?" Karlie felt her face burn bright red when her eyes snapped back up to his face. Oh my god! Had she really just eye fucked one of the campus cops standing at her door?

She fully expected to find an arrogant smirk or, at worst, a scowl when her eyes made it back to his. But what she found was an easy smile on his face. Karlie was pretty sure she could even see the hint of dimples on those shadowed cheeks.

"You called in that you were locked out?" He tried again to roust her out of her trance.

"Oh, yeah. I'm sorry." Stepping back onto the stairs, she held the door open while he stepped inside. Letting the heavy door slam closed, she turned to run upstairs. "I locked myself out of the living area. For some reason, I have to live in the room on the stairwell. The doors lock automatically so I left the keys in the kitchen when I went for popcorn." Why was she babbling? She wasn't a babbler. Socially awkward on occasion, yes, but not a babbler.

———

Max followed her up the stairs with a grin on his face. He had been headed home and had offered to take the call on his way. Coming off of an extensive stint with a gang task force, he had been temporarily assigned to a college campus for a much-needed break.

His little sister was starting her freshman year here this year so he thought it might be nice to be able to keep an eye on her. She had not been impressed when he announced he had completed the extra training to be assigned to her campus. The police force on campus was an extension of the city police but with extra certifications.

Based on the reception he just received, this could be a very good decision on his part after all. She continued to ramble the entire way up the stairs, making his grin threaten to become a permanent fixture on his face. The view wasn't too bad either.

He understood that it was hot in these apartments, but did she even realize he could see right through her white tank top? The shorts were also right out of a wet dream. With every step she took, he swore he could see the slight curve of her ass.

Karlie stopped so fast at the top of the stairs Max almost ran into her. "I feel so stupid. I'm really sorry you have to waste your time doing this."

"Don't worry about it. We get this call more than you think," he said, smiling at her. Okay, so this was the first door he had had to open, but he was sure it happened to others. She smiled shyly at him as he pulled the master keys off his belt, opening the door. "What else can I help you with?" he asked when she didn't move.

"Oh, I'm fine. It's just creepy in there and I have to go all the way to the kitchen. Better than having to climb into the Buffalo Bill basement, I guess."

"Buffalo Bill basement?" Max asked, with his eyebrows knitted in confusion. "Like the guy from *Silence of the Lambs* that was then on *Monk*?" Karlie couldn't help but laugh.

"Exactly. See, you get it. I've always wondered if he kept the nipple ring for *Monk*. That would be weird, huh?"

"I don't know," Max said, trying not to laugh. He was trying his hardest to remain professional since he was on an official call after all. "Wouldn't you be able to see it under his dress shirts?" Karlie cocked her head slightly in thought.

"Well, crap. Now I have to start watching *Monk* again. Of course, all I'll be able to focus on is Stottlemeyer's nipples.

That would be pretty badass though if the old guy on the show had nipple rings. Totally hot."

"Umm," was honestly the only thing Max could think to say. How do you respond to that?

Karlie continued to stare into the darkness of the apartment for a few more moments before taking a deep breath. "Okay, here goes. Thanks again for your help."

"Wait, I'll go with you," Max said, reaching into the room for the light switch. This was a little beyond what he was required to do but he couldn't wait to see what would fall out of her mouth next. He couldn't remember ever discussing nipple rings on a call before.

"This is... rough," he said, stepping into the living area. Who the ever living hell had been ax murdered on the couch?

"Right? It'll work, though. Last year I lived in the basement of one of the dorms, so I've already started moving my way up. Just like the song says from that old show." They continued into the kitchen, where Karlie's keys were lying on the counter.

Retracing their steps, Max turned off lights as they left each room behind until they were standing on the landing again.

"Well, I guess thank you again... Officer Scaletti," she said, squinting at the name badge on his chest.

"My pleasure, Miss James." Max tried to hide the smile brought on by the way her southern twang seemed to actually add syllables to his last name.

"Karlie," she said as her smile lit up her face.

"Max," he answered. He probably wasn't supposed to offer up his first name, but he liked Karlie. She was gorgeous, funny and obviously brave enough to stay in this pit by herself. She was also one of the students under his care and completely off-limits. Slowly he started down the staircase toward the front door. "Good night, Karlie. Sleep well."

"Thank you, Max. Stay safe," she answered. When he

reached the front door, he turned to look up. She was standing, looking over the railing at him. With a smile, he opened the door, walking outside to his SUV.

Max pulled up outside the house that had been his family home since he was a small boy. It was a three-story home, much like the one he had just left, only in much better shape and definitely in a better neighborhood.

Growing up, his father had owned an accounting business on the first floor and his family lived on the upper two floors. When his father passed away from a major heart attack Max's freshman year of high school after a long fight in the hospital with heart disease, everything had changed. The life insurance had been canceled not long after he had been diagnosed with the disease, so his mother was faced with both a large house to maintain and staggering hospital bills.

The first floor had been converted into an apartment for him, his mother and his little sister, while the other two floors were rented out to tenants. With the extra income, they were able to pay for the house expenses just leaving the medical expenses to deal with. His mother took in extra part-time work around the neighborhood until he graduated from high school and could work full time.

Talking his way into the police academy at nineteen, he convinced her to sign the forms necessary for him to join the department when he turned twenty. Making a decent salary while remaining in the house, Max was able to not only pay off most of the medical bills, but would also be able to cover any expenses not paid by his sister's college scholarship.

Max had made a good addition to the already strong police force in the area. His dark looks seemed to lend itself well since he could ease into many of the different gangs in the surrounding area. He could blend in with the Latin American gangs, Eastern European gangs, and even the Irish gangs with his working-class accent.

Unfortunately, when a slip from an informant had sent

him to the hospital the last time he was undercover with a bullet firmly lodged in his thigh, he knew it was time for a break. Campus cop for a year had seemed like the perfect escape.

"Mom, I'm home," he called out, walking into the kitchen. He still lived in a tiny bedroom in his mother's apartment while saving his money for his sister's schooling. Max figured he could survive four more years to make sure she got a degree. So, yes, at the age of twenty-five, he was a stereotypical Italian male still living at home with his mother. He couldn't think of any other way to make everything work though.

"Mom?" he called out again, taking off his uniform shirt and Kevlar vest. Walking into the living area, Max found her sleeping in her chair in front of the *Late Show*.

He was actually a second-generation American, but his grandparents had only spoken Italian when they settled into the Italian district. His parents had spoken it as he grew up, only speaking English when they had non-Italian guests over. Max, however, only spoke Italian when necessary. He gently shook his mother's shoulder until she was somewhat awake.

"Mom, why don't you head to bed?"

"Are you hungry?" she asked, standing. "I can heat you up something."

"No, I ate on campus earlier," he assured her. Giving him a kiss on the cheek, she turned toward her bedroom. One of the perks about working on campus, besides the pretty coeds moving in, was he got fed. Although the word perk might be too kind. He was still trying to hunt down something that didn't taste like organic lawn clippings.

Crossing back into the kitchen, he pulled out a bowl of his mother's baked ziti. Her cooking was the reason he had to spend so much time working out in the police gym in the basement of headquarters.

Washing his dishes, he set them on the sink's drying rack

before walking into his bedroom. He had moved into his sister's room when she moved into the dorm this week for orientation. Sleeping on the pullout sofa hadn't been too bad, but he was grateful for the extra privacy he had now.

After a quick shower, he flopped down on the small bed. He had installed new window air conditioners in the house with one of his paychecks last year, so he could at least sleep without sweating.

Max lay staring at his ceiling. Now that he was finally still, thoughts of Karlie raced to the front of his head instead of just lingering in the back where he had managed to keep them until now. He grinned, thinking about her randomly babbling about the serial killer from *Silence of the Lambs*. Who discussed nipple rings with a stranger? A police officer at that.

He definitely knew she didn't have nipple rings based on what he could see through the shirt she had on. He had checked, after all, he was a man. Just thinking about those pert nipples poking through her tank top made him hard.

If circumstances were different, he knew, without a doubt, he would have asked her out right then. But they weren't. She was a student on the campus he was assigned to, besides she couldn't possibly be older than nineteen.

He could barely remember the last time he had gotten laid. It wasn't like you could bring a woman home to your place when you lived with your mom. With a huff of breath, he shoved his boxers below his hips, wrapping his hand around his erection. Closing his eyes, he focused on the perusal down his body Karlie had given him when she opened the door and let himself go.

CHAPTER

Two

"FUGNUGGETS!" Karlie shouted at the door to her room as she stared at it from the landing. She had exactly thirty minutes to get to campus, grab some breakfast, and report to the gym. Did she really need the frustration of locking her keys in her apartment for the second time in less than twenty-four hours?

Everything was neatly packed in her team backpack for the day, except the set of keys to her apartment that were currently hanging on a hook just inside the locked door. It was the first day of practice, so she couldn't be late trying to get someone to come open her room again.

Rolling her eyes, she stomped down the stairs. She would slam the front door in anger, but since it didn't open but halfway, it was hard to get any momentum behind it.

Karlie grabbed some breakfast in the cafeteria before running to the gym in time to check in. Her morning was full of meetings that covered everything from getting sanctioned by the NCAA for betting on sports to the ramifications of hazing.

When it came time for the campus police officer to speak about what would happen to you if you were caught partying, she held out hope it would be the hot cop from last night. Nope, they sent one of the grumpy old guys for this. The campus was located where two rival gangs crossed, so they also threw in a segment about safety, especially when walking at night.

At noon, the team took a break to grab lunch together before heading back into meetings for part of the afternoon. By the time they actually got to practice, Karlie felt brain dead. How many speeches could they possibly give you about the dangers of drinking or inclusion?

She never drank in season and, as far as she knew, was nice to everyone. The volleyball team had a chance of finishing at the top of the conference this year if they focused. She had no doubt if she went to a party, the upperclassmen on her team would come drag her out by her hair.

The coach had promised an easy first workout in his email this summer, but he must have changed his mind. Karlie felt sorry for the girls who hadn't spent the summer playing sand or in the gym. As hard as she was sweating by the end, she couldn't imagine not being in playing shape still. The handful of freshmen players looked a little shell-shocked by the end.

"Karlie, want to meet for dinner in an hour?" Megan, one of the returning middle blockers, asked as they walked out of the gym.

"Sure, just let me get someone to let me back into my apartment first so I can clean up."

"Ahh, locked yourself out? I did that once. Had to get one of the university police to come let me back in."

"But did you do it two days in a row?" Karlie laughed, turning toward the small police office on campus. Walking inside, she was greeted by the nice older woman that manned the switchboard.

"Hi," Karlie said, coming to a stop when she saw Max leaning against the wall to the side of the dispatcher where they had obviously been visiting. "Umm."

"What do you need, honey?" the older lady asked. So first, she meets Max dressed in practically nothing, then she runs into him looking like something the cat hunted down, shook, ate, barfed up, then ate again. Karlie tried not to moan, thinking about the injustice of life. "Anytime today," the dispatcher said with a smirk.

"Right. I locked myself out again." She turned red, closing her eyes when she heard Max snort.

"So what do we need to do to help you remember those keys, sweetie? These officers have more to do than let you into your apartment continually."

"Yes, ma'am. But in my defense, I managed to go the entire time last year without locking my keys inside. I think it's a flaw in the current housing I'm in. I mean, why would you need three keys just to get to the bathroom?" Now she could see Max grinning out of the corner of her eye. "I should write a letter of protest to the dean about this injustice."

"You do that, honey. In the meantime, let me see who I can send over there."

"I'll go," Max said with a chuckle. "I just have to clock in, then I'll walk over with you," he added, walking toward the back. Karlie thanked the dispatcher before stepping back outside to wait for Max.

"Ready?" he asked, stepping out of the building.

"You'll probably want to walk upwind of me just to be safe," Karlie said as she slung her pack over her shoulder.

"Why is that?" Max asked, taking her pack and slinging it over his own shoulder.

"I just had practice in the gym. It was like running in a sauna, I'm sure I don't smell too good. Are you allowed to carry my bag?"

Max leaned over, taking a sniff of her neck and sending a spark of electricity down her spine. He hadn't even touched her and Karlie could feel the goose bumps rise up on her arms. She couldn't envision what would happen if he ever did touch her. She would probably burst into flames.

"You don't smell so bad. Nothing like I do after working out. Also, I doubt I'm allowed to carry your bag for safety reasons but I figured if something happens my top priority is getting you to safety. So your bag would land on the ground where I tackled you anyway. I can still shrug it off if I need to."

Karlie wondered if she slowed to an amble if he would notice her trying to drag out as much time with him as she could.

"So your first instinct would be to tackle me like a linebacker?" she asked.

"Only if I needed to cover you from a gunman. I have on the Kevlar. It can take a bullet better than the sports bra you have on."

"Speaking of boobs. The nipple ring Buffalo Bill had was fake. I Googled it." Max couldn't help laughing this time. "And now you know," Karlie added, turning red again. What is it about him that made her light up like a fire hydrant every time she opened her mouth?

"Well, I wasn't really speaking about boobs, but I'm glad I can sleep better tonight knowing that," Max agreed with a grin.

"God, I'm so sorry! I don't know why I always have to be so awkward," Karlie exclaimed, shaking her head as they reached the steps in front of her apartment. Max was silent as he pulled out the master keys to open the door. Finally turning to Karlie, he paused.

"I don't think you're awkward," he said.

"How could you not? So far I've brought up some movie character's nipple ring every time I've talked to you."

"Technically, I think I somehow brought it up this time. I did say something about your sports bra. I guess that would make me socially awkward as well?"

Karlie laughed, her eyes twinkling as she looked into his. Max grinned back. Unlocking the door, he held it open for her as she wiggled past him. She had to hold in a groan when their bodies met briefly as she wrestled through the door.

"Well, I'm glad you were around to let me in. As soon as my roommate moves in, I should be able to find her instead of bothering you constantly."

"You're not bothering me," Max answered. Reaching the second floor, he unlocked her room door, pushing it open for her. "Do you want me to check the rest of your apartment again before I go?"

Karlie walked into the room, motioning for Max to sling her bag onto her bed.

"No." She laughed, looking back at Max standing in her door. "I think the chupacabra is nocturnal anyway. He should be asleep in the basement still. There should be just enough daylight left to shower and eat."

Max chuckled, a grin lighting up his face. Karlie loved when he smiled like that. It somehow made him look younger and more carefree.

"Do you mind if I come in briefly?" he asked. When Karlie nodded, he crossed to the empty desk, pulling a card out of his wallet. Finding the pen in his front pocket, he wrote something on the card before standing back up.

"Next time you lock yourself out, call my cell number I left on the card for you. I'll swing over so you don't have to get another lecture. Or if you need me to protect you from the chupacabra. Whichever."

"I could be wrong. It could be a golem, you know. Or even Krampus. Ooh, I just gave myself the creeps." This time Max laughed loudly as he crossed back to the bedroom door. "Thank you, Max. Again!" Karlie called after him as he walked back down her stairs.

"My pleasure, Karlie. Call if you need anything." Karlie listened as the front door closed behind him.

"I'll tell you what I need, officer," she said aloud to herself as she started taking off her shoes. "I need to see what is lurking under all that Kevlar."

"I can still hear you," she heard from outside her open window. With a shriek, she fell on the bed, burying her face in her pillow in mortification. She had forgotten her window was still open and, apparently, Max was still under it on the sidewalk.

Well, now she would simply have to transfer schools. It was bad enough she always brought up nipples around him, now she had totally embarrassed herself. It's fine, she heard the circus is hiring.

———

If Karlie had bothered to look outside, she would have seen Max walk away grinning like a fool. He'd be happy to show her what's under his Kevlar, although the nasty, sweaty T-shirt he had on was probably not what she had in mind. Damn, that girl was adorable!

He knew, however, that he had to get her out of his mind. She's a student and he was on staff. It was never appropriate for them to travel in the same circle, much less become romantically involved.

Max had no problem becoming involved with someone, eventually, when life calmed down. But he didn't have time right now and he certainly didn't need to set his sights on a college student.

Max didn't officially speak to Karlie for the next two weeks. With the rest of the students moving in and classes starting, he had been kept busy.

He did include her apartment on his regular patrol route, he had watched her run to class several times and even followed her home from the gym when practice ran late. But he hadn't talked to her since he opened her door the last time.

So when he saw her sitting by herself eating lunch at one of the picnic tables in a secluded spot on campus, he couldn't help but sit down across from her with his own lunch.

"May I join you?" he asked, grimacing when he saw her jump.

"Mothertrucker!" Karlie burst out, placing a hand over her heart as if to prevent it from leaping out of her chest. Max laughed. He had missed her over the last couple of weeks.

"Sorry," he said, grinning at her. "Am I the mothertrucker?"

"You almost gave me a heart attack, so probably. What have you been up to?" Max took that as permission to join her, taking out his lunch.

"Keeping humanity safe from the chupacabras."

"Yeah, I could have sworn one followed me home from practice the other day. Wouldn't know anything about that would you?" she smirked at him as he leveled a steady gaze on her.

"I don't like you having to walk so far in the dark by yourself. It's not safe."

"Next time, just catch up and we can walk together. I like that you're there though, it gets creepy walking by myself that far." Max nodded, looking down at the bag he brought his lunch in. "Whatcha got in there anyway?"

He dumped out his lunch, looking at what his mother had packed today. He told her time and again he was perfectly capable of eating lunch in the cafeteria but she decided he was starting to lose too much weight. The result was the brown bag with lunch in it.

"It looks like it got mixed up with some second grader's," Max said, staring at the contents. His lunch consisted of a peanut butter and jelly sandwich, chips, apple, and two pudding cups. Usually, she did better than this. "What do you have?"

"Chicken Caesar salad wrap, macaroni salad, and a banana."

"Really? So you're hardcore adulting then." Max sighed, opening his sandwich.

"At least you have two pudding cups."

"True. Here," he answered, handing one to her.

"I'll make you a deal. I'll let you eat half of my salad for one of your puddings."

"Deal." They ate for a few minutes in silence while Max struggled to come up with something to talk about. He had just taken another bite of sandwich when Karlie spoke.

"Lenny Kravitz has real nipple rings. I checked. Well, not personally, although that would be living the dream. But no, I Googled it." Max managed to inhale the bite of sandwich, coughing until tears finally sprang to his eyes. "I just figured since the topic worked for us before, it might be good this time."

When Max finally managed to get the piece of sandwich unlodged from his windpipe, he looked back up at her.

"I don't know how to respond," he said, taking a drink from his water bottle. "I can assure you, though, there are no rings, nipples or otherwise under this Kevlar. That would rub like a mother." He grinned over at Karlie, who answered him with a laugh.

"No, I wouldn't imagine there would be," she said, looking thoughtful. "Well, anyway, what have you really been doing other than letting students back into their rooms?" she asked as their conversation turned to school.

He learned she was a business major leaning toward attending law school after college and he told her about attending the police academy. They had finished their lunch, reduced to scraping out the last of the pudding, when a viva-cious dark-haired beauty dropped down in the seat next to them.

"Hi!" she said, splitting a look between the two. "I know

you. You're in one of my business classes. I'm Chiara." She held her hand out to Karlie to shake.

"Karlie." Turning to Max, Karlie watched as Chiara took his pudding cup away, taking a bite from his spoon.

"I need a couple of books that aren't covered," Chiara said. Max took his wallet out, handing her his credit card.

"Just books, Chiara. Bring it back to me before I leave tonight."

"I will," she said, standing with a roll of her eyes. Handing him back the pudding, she bounced off toward the bookstore. Max watched her until she walked through the doors, greeting someone inside. Turning back to Karlie, he found her watching him intently.

"My sister," he said with a shrug.

"You work as a cop at the same school your sister attends?" Karlie asked. Max just grunted. "I bet that makes you popular at home."

"Not so much, no." He stood gathering up the trash as Karlie returned her containers to her lunch bag. After they cleaned up, Max turned to her. "Where are you off to now?"

"History class. You?"

"I have to go finish some reports, then I'm off. What time do you have practice?"

"It's done early this evening, since our first home game is tomorrow. He doesn't want us to be worn out for it. I should be back at my apartment before dark."

"Good. Well, have a good rest of your day." Max waved slightly before heading back toward the office as Karlie walked the other direction.

Walking into the building, he was greeted by one of the other officers. "Hey, was that one of the students you were sitting with?"

"Yeah, I opened her door a couple of times when she got locked out. We just happened to run into each other."

"You need to be careful. It wouldn't be good if you gave anyone the wrong impression."

"Of course. Thanks for reminding me." Max hadn't thought a simple lunch would cause a problem, but he would have to watch. He didn't need any rumors starting at their expense. This wasn't the ideal job, but he was enjoying the time off from the gang task force too much to risk it.

"So you catch the game last night?" he asked, steering the conversation toward safer ground.

Max might have been warned off of Karlie, but the idea of staying away from her and actually doing it were two different things.

The next night, he found himself standing in the corner of a full gym watching her on the volleyball court. She was fantastic. He didn't know much about the game, but he liked the fact that her jersey didn't seem to match any of the other players. It made her easier to follow as she dove to keep the ball from touching the ground.

Even though he was on duty, he made it through the first two sets before getting called to break up a fight in one of the dorms. The team had easily won the first two sets so he didn't worry about the game.

His sister had come to the game, handing him his credit card as she walked by. Chiara had invited him, somewhat reluctantly, to sit with her and her friends. It rankled him that she had looked so relieved when he had refused, explaining he needed to stay by the door in case he got a call. He had been trying to stay out of her business as best he could when he was on campus. She at least texted him to let him know they had won the final set.

─────

Karlie was covered in sweat as she helped take down the net. Her roommates had all come to the game and were waiting on her to take pictures.

"You were amazing!" Karlie heard behind her. Turning around, she found Max's sister walking over.

"Chiara! I'm so glad you came to support us."

"Max was here for a little while, but he must have gotten a call," Chiara said with a smirk on her face.

"Wait. Are we talking about your hot cop? The one that has half the campus in a flap?" Emma, one of her apartment mates, asked, walking up.

"Ooh, I've seen him. He is yummy," another apartment mate, Dana, added. "Nice job landing that."

"Guys, stop! He's not my hot cop and I didn't land anyone. All I said was he was very nice when he let me into the apartment," Karlie protested, perhaps a little too vigorously, blushing. She was still pretty red from the game, though, so she hoped no one noticed.

"Yeah, well, I saw him watching you. He is one hot piece. I'll agree with you on that," Katie, who lived in the room across the landing, chimed in. "You weren't lying there."

"Okay, gross," Chiara added, scrunching up her nose. "You know you're talking about my brother, right? The guy who can burp the alphabet?" They laughed at her description, but Karlie realized that that made him even more adorable, though in a weird adolescent way.

"Chiara, would you like to go with us to get something to eat after I clean up?" Karlie asked. There was always room for another friend. Besides, she really liked the spunky freshman.

After a quick shower, they headed to one of the local Italian restaurants in Karlie's truck. Sliding tables together, they all took a seat.

Karlie's roommate, Gemma, had decided to join them. They had lived in the same dorm when they were freshmen, so it seemed like a good decision to share an apartment the second year.

Sam, Karlie's best friend, had tagged along as well. She

lived across the hall in the other stairwell room in the apartment. They had lived next door to each other last year and had quickly become friends.

Katie, Sam's roommate, had an assignment due so she had begged off dinner. Emma and Dana, who lived in a room inside the main apartment, both had a night class, so that left Astrid, who lived in the only single room. The others hadn't known Astrid before moving into the apartment, but she was easy to live with, so they had quickly included her into their friend group.

"So, Chiara, how is freshman year going so far?" Sam asked when they were all seated.

"It's good. My roommate is crazy though."

"Trust us, we feel your pain," Sam said with a shudder, describing her freshman roommate that only bathed once a week to save the planet by conserving water. She was all for conservation, but that had been a long, stinky year.

"But enough small talk," Sam said, leaning on the table toward Chiara. "We need the inside dirt on your brother who keeps sniffing around Karlie."

"Wait, who has been sniffing Karlie?" Astrid asked.

"No one has been sniffing me. Well, just that once," Karlie answered.

"Maxim sniffed you?" Chiara asked with a mix of horror and awe.

"Where have I been? Who is Maxim?" Gemma looked around the table in confusion.

"His name is Maxim?" Sam asked at the same time.

"Well, yeah. He was named after some ancient Roman general. The name kind of freaks him out, so be sure to call him that as often as possible." Chiara looked at Karlie with a grin. "He does seem to like you, though he would never admit it to me."

"So Maxim. Huh, that's not what I thought Max was short for," Sam contemplated.

"I thought maybe Maximillian. Or Maximus, like in *The Gladiator*," Karlie added.

"How about Maximum, as in thrust or Maxum like the condoms?" Gemma said.

"I think you're thinking about Magnum condoms, but I guess it could apply," offered Sam.

"What do you think, Karlie, does Magnum apply?" Gemma teased.

"Stop!" Karlie cried. "First, you can't discuss Chiara's brother's junk in a public restaurant, especially in front of her. Second, how would I know? You can't see anything with that belt holding all the crap on it."

"So you have tried to look, at least. Simple, is it bigger than his nightstick?" Sam said, winking at Karlie. They all laughed when Chiara laid her head on the table with a groan. "We're teasing," Sam said, patting her on the back. "We promise to leave your brother's nightstick out of the conversation for the rest of dinner."

"Can I at least get the story of this hot cop up to this point? Have I seen him around campus?" Astrid asked as the pizzas were delivered. Karlie filled them in from the moment Max showed up to unlock the door to the apartment until now, leaving out the most embarrassing parts.

"Wow, that's a lot for Max." Chiara was listening to Karlie with rapt attention. "He doesn't flirt much, or ever. Our dad died when he was in high school, so he's always been too busy with work to even date. Good for you Karlie! Maybe you can drag that old man outside of his comfort zone."

"They can't date, it's against school policy. Although it would be all very telenovela like." Sam sat back, nodding her head at her assumed wisdom.

"Oh, that's juicy!" Astrid exclaimed, grabbing another slice.

"So naughty," Sam agreed.

"Can we please talk about something else?" Gemma said

with a growl. Sam looked at Karlie, raising her eyebrow in surprise. Gemma had recently had her boyfriend break up with her, so apparently men were supposed to be taboo for all of them now.

With a shrug, she steered the conversation toward other topics. It wasn't like she and Max were dating anyway. Hell, they had barely seen each other over the last couple of weeks. Besides, she knew the rules against staff and students dating were pretty strict.

It was fun to get a chance to go out with her friends. It seemed like she was so swamped between volleyball and class, she could barely claw her way to the surface sometimes.

It had been a hard game tonight, so by the time the pizza was gone, she was ready to head back to the apartment. She could really use a solid night's sleep if she hoped to make it through the rest of the week.

"Holy damn, who is that?" Astrid asked, staring out the window. Karlie looked over in time to see Max climbing off of his motorcycle in the parking lot. She only vaguely heard what was being said at the table as she watched him take off his helmet, running his hands through his hair in an attempt to coax the wet strands down. There was no Kevlar in sight this time, just his black T-shirt pulled snuggly over his hard chest.

"So he just rocketed to the top of the 'things we'd like to lick' list," Sam whispered to her, bringing Karlie back to reality. Yes, the list actually existed.

"I'm sorry, guys. I forgot to grab my wallet, so I texted Max to bring me some money to pay for my part," Chiara said with an embarrassed shrug.

"Yeah, do you hear anyone complaining?" Astrid asked with a smirk. Max walked inside, crossing to the counter where he pulled out his wallet. Karlie tried to fight the sudden urge to cause a fight when the woman leaned over, patting Max on the arm with a smile.

"Don't let that bother you," Chiara whispered to her. "She lives in our neighborhood. Max would have already hit that if he wanted to. He's not interested." Karlie smiled at her, turning slightly pink at the realization that Chiara had interpreted her twinge of jealousy correctly.

"Hi," a deep voice said behind her, making all the blood in her body heat. How could just one word make her so turned on so fast? "Chiara, I was getting out of the shower when you texted. Why are you out without your wallet?" Great! Now she was imagining him with water running down that perfect body.

Turning slightly, she found him with his arms crossed across his chest, scowling at his sister. Big, beefy arms. Damn, now she was seeing all that arm porn in the shower!

"My fault," Karlie quickly said with a small involuntary gasp when he turned his gaze on her. "We snagged her right after the game without even letting her go back to her room. If she had said something, we would have just covered her."

"Mmm," he rumbled, locking his gaze on her.

"Hello, I'm Sam." Max stared at Karlie just a moment more before looking over at Sam. Shaking her hand, he moved down the table, meeting Gemma and Astrid before moving back by Karlie.

"I caught some of your game tonight before I had to go break up a couple of dumbasses with too much weed. I don't really know anything about volleyball, but it was exciting to watch. You were amazing," Max said to her.

"Thanks," she said, sitting awkwardly, trying to pull something else out of her brain to say. Apparently she only had two speeds, talking like a nutjob or silent.

"Okay, well I'll go. It was nice to meet everyone. Don't stay out all night, Chiara. Karlie." Turning, Max walked over to the door.

"Sam, follow my lead," Chiara whispered across the table.

"Max, wait. I really need to run next door to the grocery store. Can you take me back after?"

"Seriously, Chi?" he said with a groan.

"You know, I need to go too," Sam added, picking up on Chiara's scheme. "I know you're really tired, Karlie. Would you mind giving her a ride back to our apartment and I'll keep her truck. I understand you've been there... several times," she said, giving Max a knowing smirk.

"No, I'm fine. I can wait for y'all," Karlie protested around a yawn. Max cocked his head at his sister, narrowing his eyes. She was going to protest again when he cut her off.

"It's fine, I can take you," he said, holding the door open for them.

"Great, then it's settled. Come on guys, let's walk over to the store," Chiara said, standing. She pulled Karlie up with her, dragging her to the door after Max. With a wave, the other girls quickly headed to the store, leaving Max and Karlie standing in the parking lot next to his bike.

"Umm," was all she could think to say once they were alone.

"Umm," he repeated with a smirk. "I think that's usually my line."

"So, no Kevlar this time I see," she said, making a vague motion at his chest.

"I don't wear it when I'm not working," he answered, noticeably fighting the smile that kept trying to spread across his face.

"Right," Karlie agreed, standing for a moment before reaching out to run her hands over his pecs.

"Good Jesus!" Max exclaimed, jumping.

"Just checking for nipple rings," she mumbled, turning bright red. God! What possessed her to do that? Oh, right, it was the acre of muscle staring her in the face.

"Maybe next time give me a warning?"

"Sorry, I don't know what is wrong with me sometimes."

She really didn't know. But she could at least appreciate the hard nipples now showing under the black T-shirt. Maybe she should make note of that reaction, just in case that information was needed for something in the future. Jesus, now she was even rambling to herself.

"I'm not complaining," he said, no longer fighting the grin that spread across his face. Pulling his shirt up to just above his pecs, he added, "See, no nipple rings. Do you need to check again?"

"No." Karlie laughed, meeting his eyes. "I think I'm good. Also, I can tell now, so..." Goddamn, those muscled ridges just didn't stop on his stomach. Does he even know how wet he had made her with just that one tiny view of flesh? If she ever saw him naked, she's pretty sure she would simply vanish in a puddle.

She was jarred out of her reverie when a helmet was pushed down over her head. After adjusting the straps, he slid his helmet on, straddling the bike. She stood staring at the scene in front of her, wondering how she had gotten to this point.

"Are you getting on?" Max asked, his grin making a reappearance Karlie saw through the open visor.

"Oh, right," she said, swinging up behind him. "Where do I hold on?"

"Slide against me and wrap your arms around my stomach. You can clasp your hands together if you want or you can hold on to my shirt at my ribs. Whatever is comfortable." Without a thought, Karlie gave a hard slide forward, slamming into Max. "Holy shit," he growled with a grunt.

"Sorry." She felt him move around, assuming he was trying to adjust for the passenger now smashed against his back. Sliding her arms around him, she grabbed two fistfuls of T-shirt at his waist. Trying to get settled, she opened her fist, feeling along his body for the best hold.

"Are you done feeling me up yet? I can take this somewhere private if I need to." At the gasp she let out, releasing her grip on his pecs, he laughed.

Starting the bike, Max reached back, grabbing her hands before pulling them around his stomach so she could lock her fingers. "Ready?" he shouted at her over the noise of the bike.

———

Max adjusted his erection again before pulling out of the parking lot. He had it under control until she decided to run her hands up his chest, ostensibly checking for a nipple ring. Did she want him to get one? He hadn't thought to ask that question. He guessed he could get some if she wanted. Just the thought of them rubbing against his vest made him flinch.

Although he did appreciate the reaction he had gotten at his posturing when he raised his shirt. It was a juvenile stunt, but then, he wasn't beyond pulling one if it got her attention. But then again, he wasn't supposed to be getting her attention, was he?

Stopping at one of the lights, Max reached back, patting her leg. He would swear he could feel every inch of her body shoved up against him. Fuck, he needed to stop thinking about her body before he wrecked them both into oncoming traffic.

"Are you doing okay?" he yelled over the motor. Feeling her nod her head where it was resting against his back, he eased the bike away from the light through traffic.

The restaurant wasn't far, only taking about fifteen minutes to make it back to her apartment. Pulling along the curb, Max turned off the engine. Taking his helmet off, he sat still, waiting for Karlie to unclamp her arms from around him. He wasn't in any hurry though. He liked the feeling of her wrapped around him.

"Are we there?" she asked, with her head still resting against his back.

"Yeah, sweetheart. We're there." Carefully, he held on to her as she swung off the back of the bike. Climbing off after her, he unhooked the straps holding her helmet on.

"Max," she whispered, looking at him with her big amber eyes.

"Yeah?"

"That was awesome."

"Yeah?" he asked, this time with a grin breaking out across his face.

"Yeah," she answered, smiling back at him. "It was sort of scary at first, then it was... I don't know. Just... awesome."

"Good. Maybe we can do it again sometime." Max stared down at her in the evening light, wishing more than anything at that moment he could kiss her.

He hadn't ever felt this way about a woman. Anyone in his right mind would know this was a bad road he was heading down, but he didn't care, he just wanted Karlie.

Before he could do anything irreparably stupid, he shoved his hands in his front pockets. Watching as her eyes followed his hands, he jerked them back out when her gaze settled on his crotch. With wide eyes, her head sprung up before she spun around.

"Well, thank you. I'll see you around, Max." He watched as she bounded up the steps in front of the apartment. With a small wave, she disappeared inside. He didn't move until he saw the lights come on in her room. His heart began to pound again when he saw her lean out of her window.

"Max, you'd better get home if you plan on making the world a safer place from the chupacabras tomorrow." He grinned at her, climbing back on his bike.

"Good night, Karlie."

"Good night, Max." He secured his helmet as he pointed the motorcycle back toward home.

CHAPTER
Three

MAX WAS SITTING with him mom and Chiara watching television at the end of the week when the texts began.

Karlie: Did you know you can produce enough saliva to fill two bathtubs a year?

Max: Me specifically? I didn't realize I was a drooler.

Karlie: No, not just you, everyone.

Max: I did not know that.

Karlie: Well, did you know that kangaroos can't fart?

Max: Didn't know that one either. But I'll keep that in mind if I need a roommate.

Karlie: Did you know it rains diamonds on Jupiter?

Max: Karlie, what are you doing?

Karlie: I'm on the bus playing with Siri. We had an away game tonight. We won! What are you doing?

Max: I'm watching television. Good job on your game.

Karlie: Thanks. Later. Oh, one last one. Did you know that you only dream about faces you already know?

Max laughed, drawing funny looks from both his sister and mother. He hated to tell her, but lately, her face was the only one he had been dreaming about.

Shaking his head, he slid his phone back in his pocket,

focusing on the television. His mother had made chicken cacciatore tonight, one of his sister's favorites. She had whined over the phone at him until he had finally relented and drove to campus to pick her up.

"What has you grinning so big, Maxim?" his mother asked, smiling over at him.

"You haven't heard?" Chiara answered. "Max has a girlfriend."

"I don't have a girlfriend," he mumbled, staring intently at the television. Maybe if he ignored them, they would go away.

"Really? Tell me about this girlfriend. Can I hope to hear tiny feet running around this house soon?" He caught the wink his mother made at his sister. He groaned. The woman could still dish it out. The two of them together had the ability to drive him crazy.

"Mom!" he said, sending her a glare.

"What? A mother can't dream of seeing her only son walk down the aisle?"

"I'm thinking of a spring wedding with lots of pastels," Chiara chipped in.

"Seriously, Chi, don't encourage her." He caught the grins passed between the two of them before they shared a fist bump. "And no fist bumping."

"So when do I get to meet her?"

"Probably never, since *she's not my girlfriend*." He could see them fighting off laughter out of the corner of his eye.

"Me thinks the gentleman doth protest too much," Chiara said with a nod at their mom.

"Okay, I'm taking you back," Max said with a scowl at his sister.

"Before we see if Magnum gets his man? Sweetheart, your brother is trying to break up Hawaii man candy night!" his mother looked at him in mock horror.

"Holy Christ," he mumbled.

"Maxim, I will get the soap." Rolling his eyes, he watched as the red Ferrari flew around the roads of Hawaii. The next fifteen minutes passed in blessed silence.

"So why aren't you on a date tonight?" His mother slid over at him, realizing he had finally refocused on the show.

"She's at a game," he answered mindlessly before he had a chance to digest what she had asked. "Damn it. Come on, Chi, you two get together and it brings out the worst in both of you." Both women laughed as Chiara stood up.

"I'll be back," he announced, walking toward the door, assuming his sister would follow after she had said her good-byes to their mother.

"I'll look forward to meeting her," his mother called out as he reached the back door.

"Still not my girlfriend," he yelled back, pushing outside. When Chiara finally caught up to him, he had his motorcycle started waiting on her. Handing her the spare helmet, he waited for her to get situated before pulling out from behind the house.

Fifteen minutes later, after dumping his sister off at her dorm, he found himself cruising by the field house where the bus was just pulling in. He understood that she wasn't his girlfriend. He had only yelled it at his mother no less than four times, but there was no harm in making sure she got back to her dorm safely.

The field house where the buses insisted they had to pick up was on the farthest side of campus from her apartment. It was already getting dark earlier and this campus sat in a rough area of town. It was his duty to make sure, as a campus police officer, that all the students were safe. Yeah, that sounded plausible in his brain. He would just go with that logic.

"Hey," he heard, breaking him out of his reverie. He looked up in time to see Karlie strolling toward him with her game bag over her shoulder.

"Hey. I thought you might like a ride home since I was on campus anyway." Now that he had said it out loud, it didn't seem so plausible. "Have you eaten?" Oh, that sounded even worse.

"Well, I 'ate' if that's what you call it. You know how it is when a college spends their money on academics. They produce really smart but incredibly hungry athletes." He laughed at her use of hand quotes. "I smell pretty bad though. Can't think of a lot of places that will let me in."

"Get on, I'll find something." Handing her the spare helmet, he held her backpack until she had adjusted the helmet straps. "Do you need me to swing by your apartment to leave this?"

"Nope, it'll be fine. Can we hit Taco Bell?" Chuckling, he scooted forward as she used his shoulder to pull herself up. Settling behind him, she had no problem wrapping her arms around his waist this time after securing her bag on her shoulders.

"I promise not to grope you since I'm playing big spoon back here." He roared out onto the road, the sound drowning out his laughter. Fuck, he was going to get in so much trouble for doing this.

It was really only a matter of time before he lost his shit and kissed her. Then he would get fired, his sister would have to leave and the world would explode. So maybe the world wouldn't end, but if it did, it would be so worth it.

Pulling up to the Taco Bell, he helped Karlie off, hooking her helmet on the handlebars.

"Let me have your bag," Taking her game bag, he was shocked at how heavy it was. Finding a table by the window, he set it in a chair. "Have a seat. I'll get the food. What do you want?"

"Beef tacos, please."

"Hard or soft?"

"Well, hard, of course. Soft tacos are just burritos in disguise, you know."

With a grin, he raised his eyebrows. "It seems there's a lot I don't know. I'm glad you're around to straighten me out."

Turning, he walked over to the counter, placing her order. When it was ready, he carried the tray over. "I have your tacos. I grabbed hot taco sauce, some chips with queso and cinnamon twists."

"Stop," Karlie said, holding up a hand. Max wondered what he had done wrong for a moment until she continued. "You had me at tacos." He rolled his eyes, sitting down across from her.

"Are you not eating anything?" she asked.

"I'm stuffed full from earlier. If I ate any more, I might explode." He leaned back in the chair, stretching his legs out as he watched her eat.

There was something weirdly primal about watching her eat, especially when he had gotten it for her. He thought of himself as a fairly progressive man, but this called to his baser instincts. On the most basic level, he knew he was taking care of his woman. Had he decided she was his woman? That gave him a whole new set of thoughts to work through.

"You're starting to freak me out," Karlie said between bites. Sitting up in his chair, he looked at her with concern. He didn't want her nervous around him. That sent a whole different set of thoughts racing through his brain.

"Why?"

"Because you're staring at me while I eat. I don't even think you're blinking."

"Sorry," he mumbled, standing. Picking up her bag, he set it in the seat he had vacated, taking the one next to her. "Is this better?"

Leaning over, she sniffed him, making him jump.

"Move over there," she said, pointing to the chair farthest from her. Sniffing himself, he looked at her in concern.

"Do I smell bad?"

"No, you smell amazing. That's why you need to sit over there. We don't want a repeat of the nipple ring incident, do we?" Shaking his head, he moved to the seat she indicated.

It seemed odd, but if this had been an actual date, it would have been the best one he had ever been on. Karlie never let him get truly comfortable before something crazy would pop out of her mouth. He looked forward to what would be aimed at him next.

"Officer Scaletti?" Max flinched when he heard the voice behind him. Standing, he turned to offer his hand to the man walking up to the table. "I thought that was you sitting over here. The wife sent me for something called a gordita. Surprisingly, there are not that many places that serve those in this town.

"She's expecting our fourth child," he added, looking at Karlie. "Hello, I'm Lieutenant Mason," he said, holding his hand out to her. After wiping her hands on a napkin, she took his.

"Karlie James. Very nice to meet you," she said, smiling. "I assume you're with the police department?"

"Actually, I'm Officer Scaletti's boss. The school is only borrowing him for a year while he heals up. I would guess you're a varsity athlete at the school?"

"Volleyball."

"Volleyball," he said thoughtfully. "My middle daughter wants to play. Maybe I'll bring her to see one of your games. Well, I had better get our order. If I'm gone too long, she'll turn on me." With a nod, he walked back to the counter to pick up the sack. Max nodded to him as he pushed through the doors before collapsing into the chair next to Karlie.

"Are you in trouble?" she asked, placing her trash back on her tray.

"I don't know," he answered, looking at the door his lieutenant had just disappeared through.

"Well, I'm done. You can take me back to campus where we can pretend you don't know me." Standing, she picked up her backpack, heading out the door. Taking her tray to the trash, he walked out the door after her.

"Karlie…" He wanted to say he was done pretending, but he needed his job. Like it or not, they were stuck.

"It's okay, Max. I get it, I really do." Running a finger down his shirt under his jacket, she grinned up at him. "No dame is worth your job."

"You're not just some dame," he said, rolling his eyes. Turning serious he took her hand. "I'm sorry, Karlie. I would love nothing more than to take you on a real date. It just isn't worth you getting in trouble and I've already been warned once."

Her head cocked to the side, studying him. He braced himself for what she was about to throw out.

"You'd really like to ask me out? What would we do on this hypothetical date?"

"Yes, I would really like to ask you out. Let's see, it couldn't be typical because you're anything but boring. It would have to be something pretty impressive. Maybe dinner by the lake, then a ride up the mountain to see the leaves changing. We could find a spot to spread out a blanket to watch the stars come out while sharing the hot chocolate I brought in a thermos. How does that sound?"

Reaching out, he tucked a piece of her hair behind her ear, smiling when she let out a small gasp.

"Can we do that anyway?" Karlie whispered, her eyes lighting up.

"You know you're making it really hard to stay away from you, right?" With a laugh, he helped secure her helmet before taking her back to her apartment.

Pulling to a stop in front of her door, Karlie climbed off, handing Max the extra helmet. He watched as she walked up the stairs to her porch.

"Thank you, mysterious stranger, that I have never met before, much less felt up for a nipple ring," she called out to him. With a shake of his head, he put his bike in gear.

"Christ, I am so getting fired."

———

"Has anybody else noticed that if you use this burner, your hand goes numb?" Dana asked, stirring the Jell-O on the stove.

"Let me see." Emma took the metal spoon from Dana. "Oww, it shocked me!"

"I want to try." Sam jumped when she tried to stir the concoction.

"Guys, stop. Just use a different burner." Karlie laughed at her roommates.

It was Katie's birthday, so they had decided to make a cake and Jell-O shots to celebrate. Karlie had a rare weekend off, not to mention she was the best cook, so she had volunteered to bake the cake.

They had hauled the table into the living area to give them room to all be in the kitchen. They also needed somewhere to put the food and alcohol.

Karlie had done her best to leave Max alone during the week. She saw him several times around campus but just gave him a distant pinky wave each time. It made her laugh that he couldn't stop a smile from spreading across his face every time. He never waved back, but the smile was enough.

She had almost got him in trouble again when one of the other officers he was talking to turned to look at her. She had faked indifference, but then couldn't resist a slightly rude jester after he turned back around. Hearing Max bark out a laugh before regaining control had made her day.

"What are you grinning about?" Sam asked her.

"Nothing. Why is the outside of the oven as hot as the

inside?" she asked to change the subject. She found herself grinning all the time now. Just knowing Max liked her as much as she liked him kept her cheeks aching.

"Uh-huh," Sam answered with a smirk. "Could it have something to do with being dropped off by the hot cop last week?"

"Please don't let me be too late to hear a 'hot cop' story!" Astrid said, walking into the kitchen.

"No, 'hot cop' is off-limits. Now, does anyone have any welding gloves I can use to put this cake in the oven. Seriously, feel it," Karlie answered, hunting for a hot pad. Everyone knew you had to turn the oven up really high to get it to heat at all. They had figured that out the first time it took them two hours to make a pan of brownies.

"I don't understand why we can't hash over 'hot cop?' He is the closest thing any of us have to a boyfriend," Emma pointed out, moving the pan of Jell-O over. "Do we have to keep using finger quotes when we talk about him?"

"Gemma has a boyfriend again. Besides, Max is far from being my boyfriend," Karlie said, closing the oven.

"You mean the cokehead? Yeah, he's a real winner. Max is a way hotter topic, both literally and figuratively. And yes to the finger quotes," Sam added, hopping up on the counter.

"I'm not sure he's into coke. I think it's more like acid. Doesn't matter, at least it gets her out of the room now," Karlie said.

She had gotten along with her roommate in the beginning, but the longer the semester went on, the worse it got. Gemma only left the room for class, complaining when Karlie had practice or went out with friends. Karlie didn't remember agreeing to an exclusive relationship but that was what it was starting to feel like. Gemma was simply always there.

"Whatever. Your pretend boyfriend is still better than anything I've gone out with lately." Sam was the prettiest of them all, resulting in her getting asked out a lot. The guys were rarely seen after a couple of dates, but Karlie didn't ask questions.

"Karlie, why is the oven smoking?"

"Shit," Karlie exclaimed, turning to look at the oven.

Emma had just started the second batch of Jell-O shots but was currently placing the first round in the fridge. No one had been paying attention to the stove since the cake still had a while to cook.

As if in slow motion, they all turned to stare at it in time to see a small smoke ball roll toward the ceiling. Reacting first, Karlie raced over to shut it off, receiving an impressive shock for her effort.

"Call UPD!" Sam shouted, grabbing Karlie. Pandemonium broke out as they watched the stove throw sparks.

It seemed like hours before they heard a bang downstairs, followed by the sound of boots running up the stairs. Max slid to a stop in the door, quickly assessing the situation. Turning to the officer behind him, he barked out the order to call it in, then evacuate the house.

"What did you do?" he asked, looking at Karlie.

"I tried baking a cake."

"I found a fire extinguisher," Astrid said, running back into the kitchen from the hallway, throwing it at Max.

With an impressive catch, Karlie watched Max ease toward the stove that now had billows of smoke pouring out of it. The last smoke bomb had flung the door open, causing a scream from them.

"Careful, it electrocuted me," Karlie yelled at him, making him flinch. She supposed she probably didn't need to yell when she was only a foot from him, but this had her adrenaline pumping.

"Are you okay?" he asked, scanning her from head to toe. When she nodded, he turned back to the stove. Creeping forward, he pulled the pin, angling the hose at the oven door.

Karlie eased in behind him, looking out from around his

shoulder. She was sure this would look hilarious if it wasn't for the very real chance of it ending up in death. Well, maybe not death, but a good shock was pretty serious too.

"Wait, I'll open the door the rest of the way," she blurted out, reaching for the hot pads. Before he could stop her, she grabbed the door handle, pulling the door fully open. When a fireball rolled out of the door, followed by sparks, she screamed, jumping at Max.

Landing wrapped around him, she held on for dear life as he sprayed at the stove using one hand. His other arm had wrapped around her, holding her securely to him. Hearing loud footsteps around the second collective scream from the kitchen doorway, they turned in time to see a fireman walk into the room.

"It shorted out, I think. The circuit breaker should be right outside that door," Max said, pointing at the back door. The fireman grinned at him, assessing the situation.

"Are you good?" He looked from Max to Karlie, who still clung to him. Max just shrugged as the fireman pushed past him into the alcove. Karlie picked her head up, looking at Max as she realized she had him in a very explicit death grip.

"Sorry," she mumbled, unwrapping her legs to slide down. Right then one last spark shot out at them, causing Karlie to scream, squeezing her legs back around his waist when she jumped at him.

Her momentum slamming into him had them both landing on the floor across from the demonic stove, with her straddling his waist.

"That should get it," the fireman said, returning. "We'll check for hot spots, but I think you're safe for now. Obviously don't use the stove until it's replaced." He watched Max holding Karlie, straddling his lap with the extinguisher still in his hand, before shaking his head with a grin. "Man, that never happens to me."

Laughing, he walked out of the room to speak to the other firemen.

When Max finally got Karlie seated next to Sam in the living area, he checked on the kitchen to make sure the firemen thought the apartment was safe enough to stay in.

After being assured it was the result of a stove that should have been replaced already, he spoke to the other officer, explaining that he would stay behind to write up the report. Karlie sat watching him calmly walk through the apartment, speaking to various people.

"I don't know, Kar. He didn't seem to have any problem with you straddling his hips. Are you sure there isn't something going on?" Sam whispered to her.

"Shh, he'll hear you. He has bat ears," she whispered back.

"As long as he's hung like a horse, I don't see a problem."

"Sam!"

"Karlie!"

"So, what happened?" Both girls screamed when Max spoke, standing next to them. He shook his head. Pulling the chair over, he sat down, and fished his notebook out of his pocket. "Sorry, now can you tell me what happened? You know this house is slowly racking up more calls than the rest of campus combined, right?"

He took notes as they recounted what led up to the fire. When they had finished, Sam went to her room, leaving Karlie staring at Max.

"Are you sure you're okay?" He looked her over again before moving over to the couch. "You're shaking."

"I think it's just an adrenaline dump," she answered, leaning toward him. "That was insane." Karlie couldn't have helped the giggle that escaped her lips if she tried.

The giggle turned into laughter as she took a quick look at Max. He looked back at her like she had lost her mind, making her laugh even harder. How could she not laugh, this was ludicrous. Her stove had blown up. Whose stove randomly belched fireballs? Trying to desperately catch her breath, she heard herself snort, sending her into another round of laughter.

"That's it. I'm taking you to be checked out. You're obviously in shock," Max said, standing up. Stepping between her legs, he wrapped his large hands around her biceps, pulling her to her feet. The hiccups started as she stumbled into him, making her chest hurt. Catching her with a hand around her waist, Max carefully turned her toward the stairs.

"Umm, Max?" Karlie heard Sam ask as he eased her past their rooms.

"Yeah, I don't know. I'm taking her to the clinic to be checked out," he answered, keeping a firm grip on her as they walked down the stairs, Karlie still laughing hysterically.

"Call me later," Sam called after them as Max let the door close. Karlie finally managed to get her laughing fit under control, leaving only a nasty case of hiccups and a snotty nose.

Sitting her in the passenger seat of his campus SUV, he dug around until he came up with a roll of paper towels. "Blow," he said, placing one over her nose.

With an impressive honk, she sat back in the seat with tears starting to sting the back of her eyes. Great, now she was going to start crying in front of him. It wasn't bad enough he had just wiped her nose like she was a two-year-old.

"Is this a service you offer to all of your perps?" she asked, trying to hold back the exhausted sob building in her chest.

"First off, you're not a perp. But no, just you. Well, Chiara too when she was little." He reached over her, snapping her seat belt in place before closing her door.

The drive to the campus clinic was short, even though he had to drive around campus to get there. She listened in silence as he called in that he was taking a victim in for treatment. Just hearing he thought of her as a victim started the waterworks. Karlie was pretty sure if she could just take a much-needed nap, everything would be okay.

Pulling into the parking lot, Max shut off the engine, studying her for a moment. She had pulled off another paper towel from the roll to wipe her eyes. She was positive she looked like a mess, all red and puffy, not to mention she still had hiccups.

Climbing out of his cruiser, Max walked around to her door, opening it. Looking around the mostly empty lot, he swung her legs out, stepping between them to pull her flush up against him. Well, as flush as you can get when separated by Kevlar. Wrapping his arms around her, he stood for several minutes, holding her before taking a step back.

"Come on, let's have you checked out. Someone said the stove gave you a pretty good shock. I'll wait for you in the waiting room, then get you something to eat, okay?" She nodded at him, stepping out of the vehicle.

Leading her into the clinic, he sat her in one of the chairs before walking to the counter. Within minutes, she was called to the back.

After almost an hour, Karlie had been poked, prodded, scanned, and asked a vast array of embarrassing questions. When she walked back into the waiting room, Max was standing with the doctor, she assumed discussing her.

"Everything is fine, just a small contact burn. Nothing to worry about," the doctor said, nodding at her. "Oh, those tests should be back in a couple of days. We'll email you the results." She was positive she could not get any more humiliated than she was right now. What doctor just yelled out about test results in a waiting room, especially in front of a cop?

"What test did you have?" Max asked as they walked across the parking lot. She had been wrong, it was possible for her to be more humiliated. Somehow during the hour she was being body cavity searched in the clinic, he had managed to change out of his uniform and pick up his motorcycle. He handed her the spare helmet, waiting for an answer.

"An STD test." She could feel herself turn bright red trying to pull the helmet out of his grip.

"You have an STD?" Wow, the blows just kept raining down. She watched as his face change from astonishment to disbelief to anger back to disbelief in a heartbeat, all while she wrestled him for the helmet he now had a death grip on.

"No, Max. You have to have sex to get an STD. I did finally convince them I'm not pregnant either. I guess yelling 'I'm a virgin' over and over sank in after a while. They also blew off the electrocution thing. I might die later of a heart attack but at least I won't have syphilis or crabs or whatever people get."

Karlie was yelling at Max by the end of her speech. If she didn't get something to eat soon, she would eat him. She was full-blown hangry. "What?" she yelled, watching him grin at her.

"So you're a virgin, huh?" he said with a look on his face she couldn't even begin to interpret.

"Really? After that entire tirade that was your take away? Not that I might die a painful death from the effects of electricity shooting through my body?" She didn't think it was possible to see his grin amp up even more, but it did.

"Well, at least it won't be from the clap," he said with a laugh.

"You don't know that," she said as the corners of her mouth started to twitch, holding back her own grin. "The test won't be back for two to three days."

"Why would they do all of that just because your stove caught on fire?"

"Because they are convinced that everyone that walks in the door over the age of eighteen is sexually active and riddled with disease." Max finally turned loose of the helmet, swinging his leg over the motorcycle. Reaching out, he took her arm, helping her swing up behind him.

"Well, if it's any consolation, they tested me for everything when I came out of the gang task force. I think they even covered diseases that haven't been discovered yet." When she raised her eyebrows at him, he was quick to add, "They didn't find anything. Except for that whole horse comment being accurate."

"Oh my god!" Karlie said. "How did you even hear that?"

"I do have bat ears, remember?" With a burst of laughter, he put his helmet on, starting the motorcycle.

Karlie slid on her helmet, tightening the straps before wrapping her arms around Max. She didn't know where they were going to eat, but it didn't matter as long as she was with him. The fact he hadn't run after her complete breakdown earlier, followed by an astonishing amount of overshare, made him more than just some guy she liked. It made him one of her best friends.

Feeling the motorcycle pull out of the parking lot, she tightened her grip around him, closing her eyes. He had met her with a police department sweatshirt when she came out of the back of the clinic. It was still a little cold out, but snuggling against him, she slowly relaxed.

Banging her head against Max's back in front of her, Karlie jerked awake. She had fallen asleep on the back of a motorcycle! It would have been terrifying if Max didn't have an iron grip on her. He had tucked one of her arms tightly against his side with his elbow while holding on to her other arm with his hand.

Easing the motorcycle behind a house using his remaining hand, he stopped by a back stoop.

"Hey, baby. We're here," he said softly after turning off the motorcycle.

"Where's here?" she asked as he helped her off carefully.

"My house. Are you feeling okay?"

"Did I fall asleep?"

"Yeah. I was a little afraid you'd fall off. Ready to eat?" Max had pulled her against him, wrapping his arms loosely around her back. He reached up, hooking a piece of hair behind her ear. She shivered when his knuckles brushed over her cheek as it progressed down her neck to her arm. When his hand reached her hand, he laced his fingers through hers, turning them toward the door.

CHAPTER
Four

ALL OF THE alarm bells were going off in his head. Max didn't understand what he was doing. Was the need to feed her, protect her, comfort her, and introduce her to his mom overriding every survival instinct he had?

He could have just taken her home. It's not like the school doesn't have a cafeteria. She was perfectly capable of eating there. Instead, he had texted his mom while Karlie was in the back at the clinic, telling her he was bringing someone for dinner.

"Karlie!" Max heard screamed the second they walked through the back door. Shrugging off his jacket to hang by the door, he watched as his sister threw her arms around Karlie in a bear hug. "Oh my god, are you alright? I heard that the stove tried to kill you."

"Chi, how did you get here?" Max asked, watching her rocking Karlie side to side. They hadn't even made it out of the mudroom into the kitchen yet.

"It's called a bus, Maxim. No thanks to you, I had to hear about it from Sam. She texted me saying the stove had tried to kill you. Then she let me know you had hauled Karlie to the clinic, where I'm sure they tried to blame it all on nasty sex.

Finally, Mom called to say you were bringing someone for dinner, so I hopped on a bus to be here."

Chiara finally ran out of breath as Karlie worked to unwrap herself from a grip an Anaconda would be proud of. Stepping forward to help, Max finally got her untangled from his sister, pulling her toward the kitchen.

"What is with their obsession with sex?" Max mumbled.

"Haven't you heard?" Chiara answered. "In their world, we are ground zero for all things STD."

"Right?" Karlie threw over her shoulder as they stepped through the kitchen door. "Oh my gosh, what smells so amazing?" she exclaimed, patting her stomach. Max grinned, watching her. She was so fucking adorable.

"Come in," his mother called out, walking over. "I'm Maxim's mom, Elena. We are so happy you're joining us."

"I'm so sorry to crash dinner. Max didn't tell me where we were going. Thank you so much for having me, I hope I'm not causing a problem."

His mom pulled Karlie into a hug before holding her at arm's length with a smile. "My darling, you are welcome here any time. I just hope you like my Bolognese sauce."

"If it tastes even half as good as it smells, I can guarantee you I'll lick the plate clean. Tell me what I can do to help."

"You can come sit right here while I finish. I want to hear all about you," his mother answered, pointing at the stool on the other side of the bar. "Maxim, get your girlfriend a drink."

Max opened his mouth to correct his mom when she did it for him. "Oh, that's right, she's not your girlfriend." Shaking her head at Karlie, she added, "Sometimes men are so clueless." Max felt himself turn red but Karlie was laughing, so he couldn't get mad at his mom.

He listened as Karlie visited with his mother, with lots of comments from his sister, about growing up in Texas, playing volleyball and life in her apartment. He had brought them each a water before turning to set the table. They were lucky that even though they didn't have a dining room, the kitchen had been large enough to accommodate a kitchen table capable of sitting six if the leaves were out.

He struggled to set the table with plates and silverware while often finding himself watching Karlie in a daze.

When his sister caught him once, winking at him with a grin, he turned back to the counter, opening the wine his mother had set out for dinner. They rarely sprang for wine, but his mom had gone all out with this meal, even making dessert at a moment's notice.

With dinner ready, he helped her carry everything to the table, holding out chairs until everyone was seated.

His mother asked them to join hands while he blessed the food. Taking his sister's hand on one side and Karlie's hand on the other, he marveled briefly at the difference. He had been holding his sister's hand since she was born, it always felt like a sweet gesture but nothing more.

Every time he touched Karlie's hand, however, it felt like a lightning bolt was racing through his heart.

"Maxim, turn her hand loose so she can eat, sweetie." He felt himself turn pink as he let Karlie take her hand back.

"Sorry," he mumbled. Why was he acting like he was fifteen again? He was a big, badass cop, he didn't blush from holding hands. His sister was never going to let him live this down.

"No complaints," Karlie answered, smiling at him. She looked so much better already. None of the puffiness was left around her eyes or the paleness in her face. He didn't want to tell her, but she had scared the fuck out of him back at her apartment.

It had been bad enough to get the call about a fire, but to find her standing in the middle of it while sparks shot out was heart stopping. He had fought through the panic he felt hearing she had received a bad shock, then had to keep himself from curling her up on his lap as she fell apart in front of him.

"Stop!"

"What?" he growled back at his sister.

"You know." She smirked at him. Rolling his eyes, he picked up his fork. Fine! But he was having a damn hard time not staring at her.

Most of dinner was spent with his mother regaling Karlie with stories about him growing up, much to his embarrassment. She laughed as she plowed through her food like she hadn't been fed in years.

He knew being a college athlete in season required a lot of calories that were hard to get eating in a school cafeteria. It was part of why she had wanted an apartment with a kitchen, she had told him.

"Mrs. Scarletti, this was without a doubt one of the best meals I've ever eaten," Karlie said, setting her fork on her empty plate. "Next time somebody tries to tell me where the best Italian food in town is, they're going to have a fight on their hands. Thank you."

Max watched as his mother beamed with pride at her. Damn it, he was falling hard for this girl! He already knew she was sweet and funny as hell, but what she had just said to his mom was honest. It wasn't just something said to suck up, she had meant it. Someone was getting their ass kicked over Italian food soon.

"You are so welcome. Why don't you relax in the living room while I clean this up," she said to Karlie, getting up.

"How about if you go relax while we clean up?" Karlie said, standing. "It won't take us a second, then we'll bring you a slice of cake."

Taking the dish out of his mother's hand, she turned to carry it to the sink without another word. His mother gave him an approving nod before retiring to her chair in the living room. Max put the food up while Karlie and Chiara quickly cleaned, making quick work of the kitchen. Picking up two slices of cake, Max motioned toward the living room.

"Here you go, Mom. What's on television tonight?" Handing his mother a piece of cake, he sat down on the end of the couch, patting the cushion next to him. Karlie sat down, leaving room in the other chair for Chiara to curl up.

Taking a bite of his cake, Max froze, hearing Karlie moan. He had been fighting a hard-on all night, but the sight of her eyes closed with a look of pure pleasure on her face, chewing slowly, made it swell painfully. Adjusting his seat on the couch, he tried to lessen the tightness without actually having to use a hand to fix it. He glared at his sister when she barked a laugh, watching him.

"Karlie, do you have anything you want to watch?" his mother asked her, missing him dying a slow death next to her fortunately.

"I'm game for anything." They settled on some old movie that was coming on and Max tried to relax as he finished his cake. Taking Karlie's plate when they were finished, he placed them on the coffee table in front of him. Leaning back, he discovered she had kicked her shoes off under the table, curling her feet up under her.

Within twenty minutes of the movie starting, she had slowly sunk down until her head rested on his thigh. Pulling a blanket off of the back of the couch, he covered her, resting his hand on her arm.

"She looks exhausted," his mother whispered to him as she turned the volume lower on the television.

"I think she is, Mom. Between classes, volleyball and all of the problems with her apartment, I think the stress is getting to her. She basically freaked out on me after the fire today," he whispered back.

"So, how is this girl not your girlfriend again?" she asked.

"Because," Chiara stage-whispered from her chair.

"There're rules against staff members dating students. They could both get in a lot of trouble."

"But if the circumstances were different, you would be dating?" his mother asked.

"In a heartbeat," he responded. His mother patted him on the arm in sympathy.

"It sucks," Chiara chimed in. "Karlie is really cool. She's nice to everyone, she's smart and she is a beast on the court."

Max smiled at his sister. He agreed, the rules did suck, but they were in place for a reason. He needed to remember that Karlie could get in just as much trouble as he could. He was absently running his fingers through her soft hair, pulling it gently away from her face as she slept.

"So tell me, Mom. How do I stay away from her?"

His mother looked at him with sympathy. "The heart wants what the heart wants. If this girl has stolen yours, I don't know if you can," she said.

That's not the advice he needed. He needed cold, hard rules to follow. Shakespeare now made so much more since. Crap, was he really referring to Shakespeare?

He needed to get back on the gang task force again. Sure, he had tackled a druggie wielding a knife on campus just this week, but he had obviously gone soft. It still amazed him how many people he had arrested on that campus brandishing knives.

They sat in silence watching the movie while Karlie slept curled up under the covers. The movie ended so his mom turned over to the news. He was mindlessly watching a rundown of everything bad happening in the city when his mom turned to him.

"I think you should move out," she said in a matter-of-fact tone.

"Damn, Mom. What's this about?" he asked in surprise.

"I've been thinking about it. We finally have this house paying for itself with the renters. I have a part-time job at the bakery which gives me plenty of spending money. I know you're helping Chiara with her expenses that are not covered by her scholarship, but she wants to get a campus job to help with that.

"Ida mentioned wanting to rent out the apartment above her garage so I asked if she would hold it until I could speak to you about it." Max stared at her like she had just turned into a dragon. He hadn't even thought about affording his own place until his sister had made it through college.

"Yeah, Max. Mom and I have been talking about it," Chiara said as his confused gaze swept over toward her. "The rent is cheap, so you should be able to afford it. She's also kicking in the utilities since she doesn't want to go to the hassle of separating it from her house. She said you'll have to fix it up some but I can help you."

"Maxim, you're twenty-five years old with a good job. You put everything on hold to help us. We think with" —his mom nodded at Karlie— "your life moving forward, you deserve your own place."

Looking down, he stared at Karlie, curled up, her head on his lap, loving how right it felt. If he had his own place, then maybe if she was still around when his stint on campus was over, they could start seeing each other. It would be nice to have her over in the evenings with just them.

"Okay, tell her I'll swing by tomorrow to look at it." The more he thought about finally getting to live on his own, the more excited he got about it. He would have to hunt down some furniture, but there were some good thrift stores around.

Depending on the rent, Max was positive he could finesse his budget to even spring for a few new items. Like a bed, he would definitely need a new bed. He also didn't want to buy a couch from a thrift store, but sometimes you could find one like new on Craigslist.

He looked down when Karlie moaned, thrashing her legs.

"Go put her in your bed. Chiara can sleep with me and you can take the couch. Poor thing is so tired, I hate for you to wake her up to take her home," his mom whispered at him.

"She fell asleep on the way over here. I was afraid she'd fall off the back of my bike." Easing out from under her, he leaned down, scooping her up in his arms.

With Chiara's help, he carried her into his room and laid her on his bed. Pulling the blankets up, he brushed her hair back out of her face, giving her a quick kiss on her forehead. Taking one last look at her snuggled under his blankets as he closed the door, he couldn't help feeling that this just felt so right.

———

Karlie yawned deeply as she slowly woke up. Stretching like a cat, she marveled at how much better her room smelled than it normally did. Without opening her eyes, she felt around the warm flannel sheets. Nope, this definitely wasn't her room.

Prying an eye open, she took in the furniture, the clothes tossed on the dresser and finally the utility belt draped over a doorknob minus the gun. With a groan, she flipped over, remembering where she was. Catching the time on the clock out of the corner of her eye, she bolted upright. It couldn't possibly already be ten in the morning.

Finding the sweatshirt in the corner Max had given her yesterday, she pulled it over her head. Opening the first door she saw, she quickly closed it again, realizing it was the closet. Turning in a circle, she took in the room again. She let out a small giggle, thinking about how this would be a major room-mate upgrade if this was her room.

Spying the other door, she pulled it open, walking out into the kitchen where Max sat at the table reading something on his iPad.

"Good morning," he said, looking up at her. Even in this weird circumstance, his deep brown eyes could make her shiver when they focused on her. "How did you sleep?" Watching her squirm for a few minutes, he pointed toward a door that hopefully was the bathroom.

When Karlie emerged from the bathroom, Max was standing by the microwave.

"I bet you'll be excited to get rid of me today. I seem to have turned into the guest from hell," she said with a feigned laugh. "Where is everyone else?"

She sat in one of the chairs at the table, watching him pull something out of the microwave. Setting a plate with a large cinnamon roll on it in front of her, he turned to the refrigerator. When he had poured a large glass of orange juice, he sat down across from her.

"They went to mass. No one wanted to wake you up since you were sleeping so hard, so I stayed to wait for you to wake up. But why would you think I'm ready to get rid of you?" His gaze slowly burned through her until it settled in her stomach.

"I think it would be obvious. In the span of a day, I accosted you when I blew up our stove, had a nervous breakdown, pronounced myself free of herpes, crashed your mom's dinner and fell asleep in your bed. I'm like a very bad version of Goldilocks. Being around me is courting disaster."

She stabbed into her breakfast as Max sat silently, staring at her in astonishment. She seemed to have an amazing ability to induce that look from him. She was bringing her first bite to her mouth when she heard him start to laugh.

"Maybe I like living dangerously," he said when he stopped laughing. "Or does that make me the big, bad wolf?" Karlie grinned over at him.

Max was leaning back in his chair with an arm resting over the back of it. His hair was still sticking up, but he was wearing a pair of jeans with a long-sleeve T-shirt pulled over his broad chest. She had noticed he hadn't put on his socks or shoes yet when he was standing at the counter earlier. For a moment, she wondered if it would be rude to climb over the table at him.

"Did you know in the original written version of that story, she climbs into the bed with the wolf and he devours her?" Karlie asked. How come her response to innocent flirting always had to be something weird?

Max sat grinning over at her until she finally started to squirm in her seat. "What?" she asked. With a small laugh, he sat up, looking over the table at her.

"I didn't know that. So I guess we'll wait to see how long I last before devouring you," he said, his eyes turning almost black in the kitchen light. She didn't know you could actually see lust in someone's eyes, but she decided the romance books she hid in her room were right.

She felt the redness creep up her neck as she finally realized what she had said this time. At least Little Red Riding Hood never had to sit in wet panties while being watched across the table by the sexiest wolf in the woods.

"Did I mention that sometimes when my mouth opens, words just fall out?" she asked. Max laughed, shaking his head.

"I sincerely hope it never ends," he said when he had recovered.

"Don't worry, according to my mom, it's hereditary. It comes on when we realize that boys are no longer covered in cooties."

"Oh, we're still covered, we just get better at camouflaging them."

"Is that how that works?"

"Pretty sure." They sat grinning at each other. Karlie couldn't remember ever enjoying being around someone as much as she did Max. He had a dry but wicked sense of humor and never seemed to get offended by what she said.

She wished she had known more guys like this in high school, her social life would have been so much better.

"You should probably take me home. I'm sure my room-mate will be all pissed because I didn't get my absence preap-proved." Karlie sighed. Gemma had become even more clingy lately, letting her know, in no uncertain terms, she didn't like the rumors she heard about Max. They never fought, like Sam and Katie, instead she got the whole passive-aggressive thing from Gemma.

"Problems with your roommate?" Max asked. Karlie liked that he never wasted words, just right to the point. She had enough word vomit in her to serve them both.

"I don't know. She's just always around. She doesn't like me going out if she doesn't go. Sam keeps teasing me about having my first lesbian affair. It's not true, but sometimes it feels like she's trying to isolate me away from everyone else."

"That doesn't sound good. What do you plan to do about it?"

"What can I do? I'll just make it through this year then find somewhere else to live."

"It's going to be a long year."

"Tell me something I don't know," she answered.

Max studied her for a moment. "Did you know the first American police force was started in Boston in 1838?" he asked, a smile back on his face. Karlie laughed hard before looking back down at him.

"I'm starting to rub off on you. We'd better leave quickly before you start spouting random facts about nipple rings." She stood, walking back into the bedroom to get her shoes. Sitting on the bed, she was putting on her shoes when she noticed Max standing against the doorframe.

"You know you're always welcome to stay here if things get too bad at your apartment, right?"

"Thank you," she answered quietly. When they were ready, she joined him outside at his motorcycle.

He had let her wear his police jacket for warmth since it was a cold morning. Max had found one of his old work coats in the mudroom that he had shrugged on. Climbing behind him, Karlie slid her hands under his shirt until she could feel the warmth of his skin thawing her hands.

"Fuck, those are cold," Max exclaimed, jumping when she spread her hands out on his stomach. He didn't pull them out, however, adjusting his shirt to cover them both.

For fifteen minutes, Karlie enjoyed the feel of hard, bare muscle moving against her hands as Max navigated the morning traffic to her apartment. The only thing that would have been better is if it had been a farther ride. Stepping off from behind him when they reached her apartment, she handed Max the extra helmet.

"Want to know a secret?" she asked him.

"What's that?"

"This is my first walk of shame. I didn't even do anything to be ashamed of. Thank you," she whispered, leaning close to him. With a quick kiss to his cheek, still rough from last night's beard, she turned, running up the steps.

"Glad I could be your first," she heard him yell behind her as she pushed open the door. With a laugh, she let it close. Looking up the stairs, she groaned. As much as she would like to run back outside to ride away with Max, she knew the sooner she faced the Inquisition upstairs, the better.

CHAPTER

Five

KARLIE'S WALK of shame was hardly a blip on anyone's radar thanks to Sam hooking up with some guy at a frat house party. Sam then spent part of the day fighting with Katie until Katie finally stormed out of the apartment.

Gemma did give her the cold shoulder before launching into a strained speech about how upset she was to be excluded from her and Max's activities. Karlie was hard pressed to figure out if she was upset about missing out on the STD test or sleeping in the room next to Max's mother's room.

The apartment still smelled slightly smoky from the stove fire. They also still didn't have electricity in most of the kitchen. With any luck, they would receive a new stove some-time during the next week. Someone had managed to trace the breaker that fed their fridge, flipping it back on, so Karlie didn't have that mess to clean up as well.

Grabbing her backpack, Karlie mumbled something about needing to study at Gemma before leaving to hide in the library for the rest of the day. At this point, she would sleep in the library if it meant she got a few minutes alone.

"We're going out," Sam announced, flopping down on the

couch across from her several hours later. Karlie had secured a lounge chair in the back corner on the first floor that served as a student center on campus. She had finished a Frappuccino earlier with her feet tucked up under her, reading a new fantasy novel.

"I'm in season," she answered Sam, turning a page.

"You sound like a deer hiding from a hunter. You have the weekend off. Go out with me tonight and I'll sweat it out with you tomorrow. Deal?"

Sam lay down on the couch, throwing an arm over her eyes.

"It kind of looks like you're still hungover from last night. Are you sure you need to go out tonight too?"

"What's it called? Hair of the dog? Please, Karlie?" Sam used her best whine, knowing with a little work, she could talk her into it.

"If you promise not to make that noise again, I'll go." Sam sat up, crossing her fingers over her chest in a sign of promise. "I'm starving. Can we go get something to eat?"

Glancing at her watch, Karlie was shocked to find it was already five in the afternoon. The book she chose was obviously better than she had realized. Packing up, Karlie followed Sam out of the library toward one of the main streets running past campus.

Settling on a small Thai restaurant, they found a booth in the corner.

"So, last night," Sam said, leveling her gaze at Karlie. "Rumor is you went home with the hot cop. I need to hear details."

"There aren't any details to share." Sam rolled her eyes. "I'm serious, nothing happened. His sister and mom were there, you know. The most physical activity is he apparently carried me to bed."

"Oooooh, you nasty girl." Karlie laughed at Sam's mock teasing. "Did he kiss you good night?"

"I don't think so. I was asleep but I think I would have woken up for that."

"No forehead kiss? No 'sorry I accidentally copped a feel while setting you down?' No visual displays of morning wood? No nothing?"

"It was all very sweet but very platonic. Sorry to disappoint you." Karlie grinned, mentally slapping the back of her head for forgetting to check if he had morning wood at the breakfast table. Although if she had found any, she's pretty sure she would have blurted out some stupid statistics about it.

"It's fine, that just means I'm a little closer to winning the pool."

"What pool?"

"The 'when will Max bang Karlie' pool I started last week. You have to pick a date and how it's going to happen. I have two weeks from now when he finally snaps, throwing you down on the hood of his cop car."

Karlie narrowed her eyes at Sam's smirk. It was fine, she could guarantee Sam had no chance of winning. Max was way too buttoned up to have public sex. Right? Oh god, what if he wasn't?

"The idea is freaking you out, right?" Ignoring Sam, Karlie jerked her phone out of her pocket, hastily sending out a text.

Karlie: Do you like to have sex in public?

Max: Right now?

Karlie: You can spend six months in jail if caught.

Max: Yes, I know, being a cop and all. Have you been arrested for having sex in public?

Karlie: No, I was just talking about it.

Max: With who??? Why???

Karlie: Who am I talking to or who am I having public sex with?

Max: WTF?????

Karlie: Gotta go, our food just arrived.

Max: Wait! Who are you having sex with in public?
Max: Hello?
Max: Karlie?

Shoving her phone back into her purse, Karlie laughed, hearing her stomach growl. She could talk to Max later, right now she was being reminded that she had read through lunch.

Her friends had made a rule last year that they put their phones away when they were eating together. It gave them a chance to catch up without disruptions. She always slid hers into her purse so the vibrating didn't tempt her.

"So what does everyone else have in the pool?" Karlie asked as they walked back up the hill toward their apartment having finished their dinner.

"Everything from last week in the locker room to a month from now in the bathroom at a bar. There are somewhere around thirty people in the pool. Even Chiara bought into it." Sam shrugged, huffing out a breath from the climb.

"Sam! You're going to get him fired just based on rumors."

"It's fine, besides if you'll just get with the program, I stand to win enough money to keep me in wine for a while." Sam laughed when Karlie stopped dead on the sidewalk staring at her with an open mouth.

"You're a horrible person," Karlie whispered.

"I know," Sam said, throwing an arm around her best friend. "That's why you love me."

"True dat." They continued their trek arm in arm to the apartment.

Later that evening, Karlie wandered back into Sam's room, dressed to go out.

Sam had opened a bottle of tequila that had them all in a pretty good mood. Katie had remained gone, much to Sam's relief. Gemma had a school function she had to attend so Astrid, Emma and Dana were the only ones left in the apartment. Sam had harassed them all until they had agreed to come.

By nine, with an impressive tequila buzz, they all headed out to meet the car they had ordered.

"Welcome to my newest discovery," Sam announced when they all piled out of the car in front of a pub named Donnelly's. With a whoop, they followed Sam in the door, finding a large table the farthest distance from the bar.

"Hello, welcome to Donnelly's," a pretty young waitress greeted them when they were settled. "Afraid you were spotted walking in the door. The men at that table sent you a round." She motioned with her head to a table of men while setting the drinks down in front of them. "Can I bring you something to eat?"

"How about whatever the chef recommends for appetizers. Just bring us a couple to share," Sam said, nodding at the men ogling them from the other table. "Oh, and at least one without any meat on it."

"Coming up," the waitress said, turning back toward the bar. They said a toast, clinking their shot glasses together before downing them. It didn't take long for another round to show up, purchased by a different table.

"I like this place," Astrid said. "The men are so generous." They all laughed.

"Yeah, I'm sure they will be more than happy to show you how 'generous' they can be later," Sam laughed. "I love this place, it's so hometown, you know? Have any of you checked out the bartender yet? He is all kinds of bad boy hot."

As if they had choreographed their movements, they all turned to look over at the bar. "No, no, don't look. He's already busted me for having a fake ID once."

"He's super hot. Have you hooked up with him yet?" Dana asked Sam with a slight drunk slur. "I mean, you're so pretty."

"Ahh, thank you Dana. I love you guys," Sam answered.

Through Karlie's buzzy haze, she knew when they started heartfelt expressions of love, it was probably time to switch to soda. At this point, coffee might be an even wiser choice.

Right as she was trying to regain that thought, the waitress set down a tray of appetizers accompanied by another round of shots.

They were, without a doubt, rocking it tonight. Looking around the table, Karlie smiled at her roommates in turn. Considering how yesterday had gone, she couldn't have planned for a better Saturday than the one she was enjoying right now. The only thing that would make it better was Max.

————

Max watched from a block away as Karlie and the rest of the roommates loaded into a car dressed to go out. He had been on his way over during his break to demand what the heck her last text was about. Who texts someone asking about sex in public then not answer back?

He had to work the evening shift, which always resulted in twice as many calls on a Saturday night. If he wasn't on duty, he would just follow them to see where they were heading. Pulling out his phone, he sent off a text to his sister.

Max: Do you know what Karlie's plans were tonight?

Chiara: No. Why?

Max: No reason, I just saw her leaving campus.

Chiara: Were you stalking her?

Max: No?

Chiara: Were you standing outside her apartment watching her?

Max: I'm on patrol tonight. I saw her leaving with her roommates.

Chiara: That's called stalking, Max. Stop being a creeper.

Rolling his eyes, he slid his phone back in his pocket. He

wasn't stalking Karlie. Was he? No, it wasn't stalking if she started it by asking public sex questions.

Turning around, he headed back over to the office. It was probably for the best that she was out tonight. That way, he wasn't tempted to check up on her again or break into her apartment and drag her out to show her his idea of public nudity. You know, whatever.

But what if they met up with someone that tried to pull something on her? Did she have her phone so she could call him to come save her? Fuck, now he thought he was some protector looking to save her virtue. Well, that wasn't completely right. He would happily destroy her virtue, apparently in public.

With a roar of frustration, he held out his hand, palms out, to the students who had jumped in fear at the noise.

"Sorry," he mumbled as he walked past them. At this rate, he would have a wicked case of insanity by the end of the night. When his phone vibrated in his pocket with an incoming text, he stopped, fishing it out.

Chiara: Do you want to meet me for food?
Max: Sure
Chiara: Bistro in ten?
Max: Fine

Changing his route, Max checked his watch to make sure he still had time for something to eat. Walking into the bistro on the first floor of the library, he sat at one of the high-top tables to wait for his sister. Checking his phone again, he ground his teeth together, finding nothing recent from Karlie.

"Max!" Chiara called out, giving him a kiss on the cheek before sliding onto the seat across from him.

"I thought you didn't want to be seen with me around campus?" he growled at her. Chiara grinned at him before standing back up.

"That was before it got around campus that you're seeing

the star libero on the volleyball team. What do you want?" Pulling his wallet out, Max tossed some cash on the table.

"I'm not seeing anyone," he said a little too loudly, drawing looks from the other tables. Why were there this many students in the library this late at night anyway? Didn't they have a party somewhere they should be getting shit-faced at? "Coffee and whatever Danish they have left."

"Someone is in a mood," Chiara said, sitting back down with their order. "What's going on?"

"Nothing's going on. You asked me to get something to eat, remember?" Max sat back, looking around the room while he sipped on his coffee. When his gaze returned to his sister, he found her watching him with a smirk. "What?"

"Max, seriously? You're obviously crazy about her. I mean, you brought her home last night, then let her stay in your bed. Why are you fighting this so hard?"

"Chi, keep it down." Max looked around, making sure no one had been listening. "She's a student, there can't be anything between us. I could get fired, but worse, she could get suspended. Affairs aren't tolerated between staff and students."

"Then why do you keep hanging around her?" Chiara leaned toward him, resting with her arms crossed on the table. She waited patiently while Max looked around the room again, trying to put into words why he couldn't stay away from her. How was he supposed to explain it to Chiara when he wasn't even sure himself? Finally, his gaze returned to her again.

"I don't know," he said, resignation laced through his face. "She's so funny, I laugh all the time when I'm with her. She throws these crazy random facts or topics at me that I can't even hope to keep up with." Chiara sat perfectly still, listening to Max. He could see the concern in her eyes as she watched him. "It's like, when she's in trouble, no one can take care of her but me. Does that make me insane?"

"I think that makes you in love," Chiara said quietly.

"How could I be in love with someone I haven't even kissed? It's ridiculous." He stared down at his coffee cup to avoid her eyes.

His sister was wrong, it was more than just love. He wanted to spend every second with her, he wanted to be the one she turned to when she was in trouble and, damn it, he wanted to know where she was right now.

With a sigh, he stood up.

"I should get back on duty. Come on, I'll walk with you back to your dorm." Chiara stood up as Max tossed their trash away. When he turned around, she wrapped him in a bear hug, which was never easy to do around the Kevlar.

"I love you, Max. Don't give up, she won't be in school forever." With a squeeze, she stepped back to head toward the door.

"I love you too, Chi," he mumbled, following her. Within five minutes, he had her back to her dorm. With a wave, she ducked inside while he continued around campus.

Using his radio to check in, he looked at his watch with a groan when he realized he still had several hours to go. He'd just make a pass by Karlie's apartment to see if she was back yet, it was part of his patrol after all.

After a brisk fifteen-minute walk, he had reached her door. The light was still out in her room, so he checked Sam's window, finding it also dark. With a growl, he spun around, heading west, back onto campus.

It was almost the end of his shift before he heard from Karlie.

Karlie: We're having a fight over who has the best ass. I say it's you but Astrid says the bartender. Can you send me a picture of your ass?

Max: What? Where are you?

Karlie: Max!!! I need your ass!!!

Max: Where are you?

Karlie: Shhh! The bartender might have nipple rings. I'm going to find out for you.

Max: Karlie! Don't grope the bartender.

Karlie: Psst! Can I tell you a secret? We're not supposed to be drinking but these men keep buying us shots when Parker isn't looking. You know what else? Parker doesn't say his rrrs always. I might need to throw up.

Max: Karlie?

Max: Don't leave. I'm coming to get you.

Max had gotten to know a lot of the bartenders in town during his time on patrol. As far as he knew, there was only one named Parker. He worked in a bar called Donnelly's in the old warehouse district. He remembered Parker as being one of the more conscientious bartenders when it came to serving underage patrons.

Getting permission to leave a few minutes before his shift was over, Max jogged out to his motorcycle. Racing out of the campus parking lot, he headed downtown.

The first thing that hit Max when he walked into Donnelly's was the noise. Even for a Saturday night, the place was packed. Fighting through the crowd, he finally saw the table Karlie was sitting at. Weaving over, he stopped at their table with a scowl.

"How in the hell did you get served here?" he growled, looking around the table. They had the decency to at least look slightly chastised until Karlie started to giggle.

"You could have just sent a picture of your ass, you didn't have to bring it down here." Reaching over, she grabbed a handful of Max's ass, making him jump back.

"If you are one of the assholes buying them shots to get in their pants and whatnot, I will throw you out of this bar myself," a man growled, walking up behind Max. Turning around, he came face-to-face with a very harried-looking Parker.

"Wait, I've seen you before," Parker said. "Didn't you

come in here a couple of times? You're a cop, right? Doesn't matter, get away from them." The bartender leaned over, setting cups of coffee down in front of the girls.

"You can have cream in your coffee, but nothing else. Do you hear me?" Standing, he eyed Max. "I'm not shitting you, move on."

"Parker without the rrrrs," Karlie slurred with a grin. "Max, this is Parker. Parker, tell him how you say your name, it's so funny."

"Sweetheart, do you know this guy?" Parker asked her, eyeing Max.

"Yeah, he's my hot cop."

"Fuck. Tell me you're not here to bust my ass. I've been trying to deal with them, but I can't keep an eye on them and the bar at the same time. The sharks are pretty deep in here tonight."

"No, I'm not here to bust you. I came to see what I needed to do to get them back to their apartment."

"Oh my god, I just thought of something. Max, you, and Parker turn around and stand next to each other. Astrid, I'll bet you a million dollars that Max's ass is better than Parker's," Karlie slurred, drawing squeals from the other women as they leaned forward, ready to cast their vote.

"Yeah, they've been like this half the night. If you can keep an eye on them until the game crowd thins out, I'll help you wrestle them into a car. I'll keep Andrea filling their coffee cups. What can I get you?"

Parker half turned to return to the bar, waiting for Max to answer when someone bounced a quarter off of the bartender's ass.

"Coke is fine. Let me know what the damage is. Karlie!" Max exclaimed, grabbing her hand off his ass. With a laugh, Parker headed to the bar.

Turning around, Max pulled Karlie up before resettling her on his lap, since there were no extra chairs. She wrapped her arms around him, giving him a big, sloppy kiss on the cheek before settling against his chest.

"Isn't he pretty?" she asked her friends, looking around. "You should feel his abs. Really feel them," she said, laughing as Max caught Emma's hands before they could land on his stomach.

"He's yummy, Kar. But remember, you have to wait two more weeks." Sam nodded with a knowing smile, drunkenly grabbing her coffee with both hands before raising it to her lips.

"This doesn't have any Bailey's in it. Didn't Parker promise us Bailey's if we behaved? I haven't felt him up in at least twenty minutes." She stuck her lip out in a pout, complaining to the table.

"Barkeep, where's our liquor?" Dana called out as they all burst into hysterics.

"How much have you had?" Max asked, looking around the table. "What happens in two weeks?"

"We haven't had that much, sir. I have tomorrow in the pool, with Colonel Mustard in the library." Astrid held up her coffee cup in salute to the table before they all started another round of laughter.

"It's okay, Maxmum, Maxium, big guy," Karlie slurred, patting on Max's chest. "They have a pool going on when we'll have," she lowered her voice to a stage whisper. "S-E-X." Letting out a loud belch, she slapped her hand over her mouth in shock before the next round of giggling started.

"That's ridiculous," Max mumbled, shaking his head. "Who started a pool about us?"

"Your sister bet on next week," Sam added before adding a belch of her own to the fray. Max listened to them talk until the coffee finally started to kick in. When their banter turned into yawns, he knew it was time to get them home.

Catching Parker's eye, he motioned the man over to the

table. Walking over, Parker waved to a couple leaving the bar as he stopped next to Astrid, whose head was on the table.

"You ready to haul them out of here? I bet they feel good tomorrow." Parker grinned, looking around the table.

"Yeah, I'm glad they can sleep in at least. Can you help me get them into a car, I can come back for my bike later."

"Sure, man, I'll just have one of my brothers push it around back so you can pick it up tomorrow if you want. It'll be safe back there. No one dares mess with my stuff.

"You used to come in here with my cousin, I remember now. Makes sense why that idiot got sent to the pen now. Come on, let me help." Parker motioned for his older waitress to watch the bar for him while he helped. The bar had emptied out steadily for the last hour, so there was a clear path to the front door.

Standing, Max wrapped an arm around Karlie while reaching over to pull Sam out of her chair. Fortunately, she was stable enough to walk on her own after he had her steadied. Wrapping his other arm around Emma, Max started to the door, followed by Parker holding Astrid and Dana.

Helping Karlie into the SUV Parker had called, Max slid Emma into the back seat before turning around to help Sam plop down next to Karlie. When he had everyone loaded with Parker's help, he shook the bartender's hand.

"Just so you know," Parker said, "next time they pull a stunt like this, I will call the cops. Let them know if they want to get this drunk again, to do it at home." With a nod, Max climbed into the seat next to Sam for the trip back to their apartment.

He didn't blame Parker at all, this stunt could have cost him his license if they had been caught. When they sobered up, he would make sure they understood what a favor Parker had done for them trying to handle the problem himself.

Getting the crew upstairs to their rooms proved to be harder than he had realized. It took several trips hanging on to each one so they didn't chance a tumble back down the stairs. When they were each in a bed with a trash can next to them, Max slumped down on the couch. Fortunately, the other two roommates were still out, so he didn't have to worry about waking anyone up.

Pulling himself off the couch, he checked that the apartment was secure before calling for a car to take him back downtown. True to his word, Parker had stowed his motorcycle around the back by an old Dodge Ram Charger.

Firing it up, he drove home quickly, falling asleep almost as soon as his head hit the pillow. The last memory he had before drifting off made him laugh. It was Karlie, snuggled up against him, spelling sex in his ear. He was glad she had been too drunk to notice that just the word rolling out of her mouth made him hard enough to pound nails.

With a grin, he drifted off.

CHAPTER
Six

"DID you know that you can't drink alcohol in British Parliament unless you're the chancellor during his budget talk?" Karlie asked, sitting down across from Max at the picnic table he usually ate lunch at now. He looked over at her with his eyebrow raised in question. She hadn't seen him in several days, only receiving the obligatory text to check on her well-being.

No one would blame him for being mad at her. When they had gone the next day to apologize to Parker for their actions, he had filled them in on their behavior around Max. She couldn't believe she had let loose a whole diatribe on his ass. It was a really great ass though.

She watched him stare off at campus for a few minutes before setting his sandwich down on the bag he had brought his lunch in.

"Did you know a gin and tonic will glow under a UV light? The tonic contains quinine, which reacts with the light," he said, still looking off. With a sigh, he reached into his bag, pulling his extra pudding out for her.

"I'm sorry, Max," Karlie said quietly, wrapping her hand

around his holding the pudding out to her. She turned it loose when his gaze finally swung around to meet hers.

"Karlie. That was dangerous. Not just to you, but to everyone involved. Parker could have lost his license."

"I know," she said quietly, fiddling with the pudding cup. Reaching over, Max peeled the top back, setting it back down in front of her with a spoon.

"We've already apologized to Parker. I just needed to find you to say I'm really sorry. If it's any consolation, Sam made me sweat all of it out the next day. I was all kinds of ugly." She let out a small sigh when he finally smiled.

"Nothing you do could ever be ugly," he answered, shaking his head. Standing, he packed up the remaining lunch, tossing away his trash.

"Also, for the record," he said with a smirk. "I don't do sex in public and my ass is way better than Parker's. Now pay attention in case you missed it the other night." Karlie laughed as Max pointed to his ass before strutting off toward the university police office.

Sliding into the seat next to Karlie at the picnic table, Sam snatched up the pudding cup as she watched Max walk away. They had agreed to let Karlie handle this apology, since Sam had to be the spokeswoman to Parker.

He had been amazingly good-natured about the whole thing but warned them not to do it again. He had also insisted that Karlie give him Max's number for next time before informing them that no cop had even half as good an ass as him.

"So is he pissed?" Sam asked Karlie when Max had disappeared from sight.

"Not too bad. He doesn't seem to get that riled though. Hey!" she said, taking her pudding back from Sam.

"If you're too busy fantasizing to eat it, I'm going to."

"It's not like I can *not* watch his ass when he walks off. I don't have that kind of willpower."

Finishing the last of the pudding, Karlie stood up, crossing to the trash can. "I have to go to class, then practice, so I'll see you tonight." With an impressive hook shot, she launched the cup into the trash before it shot back out at her, followed closely by an angry squirrel.

"Crap on a stick!" she screamed. Placing her hand over her heart, she shook her head at a laughing Sam before walking away.

Those damn things would be the death of her someday. They always seemed to have a mouthful of food when they popped out of the trash cans. It was probably why they were the size of houses.

Karlie made it to her class right before the instructor walked in. She was a business major but every semester the school had a guest instructor teach a prelaw course. Registering for the first one last semester, she had chosen it simply because it fit into her schedule. But she had enjoyed it so much, she was now thinking about law school.

The instructor was an older defense attorney that was teaching a basic course on criminal justice and community law. She had researched his firm shortly after classes started.

Simms, Burns, and Mercer had an impressive record for acquittals and reduced sentences for their clients. She had enjoyed Mr. Simms's lectures so much that she almost had Sam talked into taking his class next semester with her.

After class, Karlie had a grueling volleyball practice. If they continued to play as well as they had been, there was a very good chance they could finish at the top of their conference this year. It was already guaranteed they would compete in the conference tournament at the end of the season again.

When practice finished, Max wasn't there to walk her to her apartment but there were two other police SUVs to escort them through the dark so his continued hammering on his boss about their safety had succeeded.

Climbing the steps to her apartment after practice made

her sigh. Of course her roommate would be there, she was always there. The only question was if she would be greeted with the passive part of their relationship or the aggressive part.

Finding her roommate listening to her headphones on her bed when she walked in, Karlie grabbed her stuff, heading for the shower. When she returned to her room, the lights had been turned off. Was this the passive or aggressive part? Who knew anymore, who cared?

Flopping down on her own bed, she put her earbuds in, pulling up the music app she subscribed to. Noticing a text from Max, she chose her playlist before opening her messages.

Max: Did you make it home okay?

Karlie: I had a police escort. Was that your doing?

Max: They volunteered. We just want all of you to be safe. What are you doing?

Karlie: Listening to music while being ignored by my roommate. You?

Max: Not much. What are you listening to?

Karlie: Jazz.

Max: Interesting but not surprising.

Karlie: ???

Max: You're a conundrum wrapped in a contradiction sprinkled with unpredictability. Of course you listen to jazz.

Karlie: Wow! That sounds bad.

Max: Actually, it's perfect. Lunch at the table tomorrow?

Karlie: Why, Max, are you asking me on a date?

Max: Shh, we're not allowed to date, remember? I'll bring lunch. Lasagna okay?

Karlie: Okay? I just had a mini mouth orgasm.

Max: Now I have to go take another shower.

Karlie: My bad. Night, Max.

Max: Night, Karlie.

Karlie lay back on her pillow with a grin on her face. She knew Max wouldn't stay mad at her, but it was nice to see them back on steady ground.

There was little doubt in her mind that, if circumstances were different, they would be officially dating by now. Three more years wasn't really that long, but right now, it felt like a lifetime. She could wait for him, though. She would have to. Somewhere deep inside, she knew Max was it for her.

———

Max set his phone back down, picking up the paint roller. He had finished the living/kitchen area in his new apartment yesterday and had moved on to the bedroom. The guy at the store suggested he stick with a light color to make the apartment look bigger than it actually was.

He was excited to show Karlie his new place, but he wanted it to look finished when he brought her over the first time. Laughing at himself, he worked more of the paint up the wall.

He had always assumed he would find someone eventually. Eventually being the key word. But never did he think he would be taking up with a college-aged, volleyball-playing firecracker. It was actually possible he could be married to a lawyer someday. A lawyer, for Christ's sake!

"The bathroom is officially cut-in," Chiara said, walking into the bedroom. "What next?"

"I should probably take you back. It's getting late." Max set the roller back in the pan.

"It's cool. I don't have class until after lunch tomorrow. This place is starting to look good," she said, looking around the room. "When are you showing Karlie? Oh, please, don't even try to hide it," she added when Max opened his mouth to protest.

After a moment, he sighed, walking into the kitchen with

Chiara on his heels. Pulling two beers out of the fridge, he opened them, handing one to his sister before sitting on the couch. He had bought it for a song from one of his mom's friends who was downsizing.

"Yeah, you're right."

"Of course I'm right. I'm a master of omniscience." Max laughed, shoving Chiara with his hand.

"Whatever. I'd like it to look a little more put together before she sees it."

"I've never seen you primp this bad for any other girl. Someone has an extreme case of the likes. This place already looks like a palace compared to where she lives now. Someone's building himself a love shack."

Max tried his best to scowl at Chiara but it was almost impossible to do with a grin on his face. "You're such a brat," he laughed.

They polished off the remaining brownies their mother had sent over earlier, before he took her back to the dorm. Cleaning up the paint when he returned, he finally fell onto the couch sometime around midnight.

Chi had accused him of having an extreme case of likes. That was a pretty accurate description of how he felt about Karlie but he knew it wouldn't take much to push him over the cliff.

Max hadn't ever truly been in love. Sure, he had the same crushes on girls growing up that others did. He had even dated several through the years, losing his virginity in late high school.

But this was the first time he could remember his heart hammering in his chest every time he looked at his phone to see it was Karlie texting him. He couldn't think of any other person that made the world disappear from view every time he saw her walking across campus.

Figuring out why it was like that was impossible, he had tried. He had even tried to control this visceral reaction to no avail. All he knew was that somewhere deep inside him, she was it for him. Through a strange twist of circumstances, she had been put in his path and he wasn't questioning fate anymore. He just had to keep his head on straight until graduation, then nothing would keep him from her.

His heart put him through its paces again the next day when he saw her waiting at the picnic table they had started eating at together a couple times a week. He had packed two bags with their lunch, one hot and one cold.

He thought his stupid heart would leap out of his chest when she looked up, catching his eyes, a smile spreading across her face. Would he ever get where he didn't break into heart palpitations when he saw her? He wouldn't have to work on cardio soon, his body was going to take care of it for him.

"Hey. I was so excited to see what you brought, I got here early," she said as Max set everything down on the table before opening the first bag.

"I hope you're hungry, there's enough for an army in here." Pulling out each item, he opened it, setting it in front of them.

After unloading the lasagna and bread, he pulled open the other bag, adding small salads and dessert. Finally, he opened two bottles of water, knowing Karlie didn't drink caffeine often during her season and handed her the silverware he had brought.

"Maxim Scaletti, did you bring me real silverware instead of plastic? We're on a fancy *nondate* date," she ribbed him good-naturedly.

"Only the best for my nondate."

"Oh, oh Max," Karlie moaned, closing her eyes after taking a bite of the hot lasagna. "So good." He stopped with his first bite midway to his mouth at her moan, feeling himself go instantly hard. "I need more," she growled, swallowing her bite.

"Holy fuck," Max mumbled, adjusting himself under the table.

"What?"

"You can't make those noises, it makes me hard," Max said quietly, looking around them. Without warning, Karlie's hand shot under the table, cupping him for a moment before pulling away.

"Yep, that's pretty big."

"Jesus, you're supposed to warn me. Remember?" Max said, jumping before a grin broke out on his face. "Big, huh?" Karlie rolled her eyes at him with a snort of laughter.

"Well, not that I have a lot to compare it to, but sure, it seems pretty big. Maybe I need to see more samples," she said with a wink. "I wonder what Parker is up to today."

"Hey! No checking out the bartender's junk."

"I was just trying to give you an accurate assessment of your...attributes."

Max laughed, shaking his head. "Life with you will never be dull, will it?" he asked, taking his first bite.

"Psst, anybody can do dull. It takes special talent to be this inappropriate on a recurring basis." They both took another bite, smiling at each other.

When he had swallowed, Max leaned toward Karlie. "Can I let you in on a secret?" he asked. "I like your inappropriateness."

She grinned back at him and he struggled to remind himself why he couldn't kiss her like there was no tomorrow while sitting at this table.

They finished their lunch while comparing campus stories. Max told her about some of the crazier calls he had been on while Karlie regaled him with more stories of the apartment. He hated that her relationship with her roommate had become strangely hostile, but there wasn't anything he could do about it.

After helping clean up their lunch, Karlie said goodbye

before heading toward her afternoon class. Max walked back to the office to store the bags in his locker. After checking in, he headed out to patrol the campus, finding it impossible to fight the grin on his face that only being with Karlie could put there.

CHAPTER
Seven

HALLOWEEN HAD FINALLY ARRIVED, turning the air cold as the last of the trees lost their leaves. Playoffs were right around the corner, but for tonight, Karlie had decided to head out with her friends.

A newer stove had been hauled into their apartment, making tonight's Jell-O shots possible again. The walls were still a little smoked up, even after they had tried to clean them, but so far things had evened out somewhat in the apartment.

"What do you think?" Sam asked, bouncing into Karlie's room, dressed for the night.

"Are you aiming for slutty Army brat?" Sam was wearing a pair of tight camo pants she had cut into Daisy Dukes, coupled with a military-style shirt unbuttoned to show her cleavage dramatically enhanced by her pushup bra. She nodded vigorously at Karlie with a wicked grin. "Then I'd say you nailed it."

"Speaking of getting nailed, has Max seen this outfit? There would be no way for him to keep his hands off you, rules or no rules."

Karlie had pulled one of her old private school plaid skirts out of one of the storage boxes. One of the white mono-grammed shirts tied at the waist and a pair of cheap saddle oxfords turned her into something out of an Aerosmith video.

"Boom! I'm ready," Astrid announced, jumping into Karlie's room with her hands above her head. Both Karlie and Sam stared at her in amazement, wondering if Astrid would ever stop surprising them. "That's right, bitches. I was a high school cheerleader."

She had on a cheerleading outfit complete with short skirt and snug sweater with letters on the front. When she spun around and bent over, they could actually see bloomers underneath, since the skirt was so short. She also had her hair in two ponytails, with a large bow in each one.

"Holy shit, Astrid. Who are you?" Sam said with a teasing laugh.

"She's the third Charlie's Angel of this male wet dream," Karlie added with a hip bump to Astrid.

"I've got to grab my pom-poms on the way out the door. Oh, I also told Chiara she could come with us. I hope that's okay." Astrid flopped down in the beanbag to wait for her friends to finish getting ready. Karlie had grown to really like the quiet girl from New Jersey.

"Who else is going with us? I know Katie is with her slea-zoid boyfriend," Sam said, joining Astrid on the beanbag.

"I think Gemma was going to a party on the other side of campus." Karlie bent over to tie her shoes as she ran down the list of flatmates. "Emma has to work tonight driving the campus escort van and I think Dana went home for the weekend."

"Chi says she should be over in around fifteen minutes," Astrid said, looking at her phone. "Just enough time for a round of Jell-O shots!" Crawling her way out of the beanbag, she headed to the kitchen. Sam grinned at Karlie as she put on a headband to pull her hair back.

Each taking a cup from Astrid when she returned, they

worked at sucking down each shot of grape gelatin infused with vodka. "Chi's downstairs."

"Let's do this!" Sam shouted, leading them down the front stairs, where they joined Chiara at the front door. Karlie was so excited to have a night off. She knew she couldn't drink much with playoffs starting next week, but she could still dance her ass off.

They had agreed to start the evening at a party her teammate, Lauren, was throwing at her apartment. It was two blocks from campus, but wasn't part of the university-owned housing. When they arrived, they found the party in full swing, full of students in costume.

"Hey, guys!" Lauren yelled over the music. "Drinks are in the kitchen, food too." Karlie gave her a hug as she followed Sam through the door. Sam placed their offering of tequila in the kitchen next to the other bottles. It was understood that the parties around campus were BYOB to help defray the cost.

Before Karlie knew it, she was dancing with Astrid in the living room in the middle of a crowd of other students while Sam chatted up one of the soccer players over the keg.

She had texted Max earlier tonight, knowing he was working somewhere around campus. Anybody who had to work at a college campus during Halloween usually had a crappy night, but he had sounded good from what she could tell.

"Are we about ready to move on?" she heard Sam ask in her ear a couple hours later while dancing behind her. "I just heard about another party that is supposed to be just a couple blocks farther down the street."

"Where are Astrid and Chiara?"

"Dancing together on the other side of the crowd. Don't worry, Astrid has kept an eye on Chi. None of us want our asses kicked by your boyfriend."

"He's not my boyfriend."

"Sure, tell it to this crowd. Have you wondered why the guys have kept a wide berth around you." Now that Sam had pointed it out, she had only danced with other women most of the night.

"We've had to threaten a couple of the baseball players about Chi though. Dressed like that, she is fair game," Sam added. Chiara had shown up at the apartment in a full catsuit complete with ears. It covered her body, but left very little to the imagination.

"Okay, let's check out the next place. You grab them, I'll say bye to Lauren." Parting ways, they both fought through the crowd until finally meeting back up outside. Looping their arms through each other's, they started the hike to the next party.

"Look, I got five phone numbers." Chiara laughed, showing them the wad of napkins in her purse.

"Any of interest?" Sam asked, holding up an equal amount of numbers.

"Maybe, we'll see. Several were seniors, so no, to those. I mean, I'm not stupid, I know what they're after."

"Smart girl," Sam agreed, beaming at Chiara. "Max would be proud."

"Speaking of my brother," Chiara said. "Can we not mention I went partying with you guys tonight to him. He's riled up enough at the thought of Karlie out, I think both of us would push him over the edge."

"Oooh, spill the chisme, Chi. How horny is he for our girl?" Sam spit out with a grin.

"Sam!" Karlie said with a groan.

"Well, I can tell you this," Chiara leaned toward them in true conspiracy fashion. "If he doesn't do something soon, he's going to explode. He's becoming completely psychotic." They laughed as Karlie turned red.

"You are all terrible, terrible, terrible, terrible," Karlie said in her best Charles Barkley impersonation. "Look, y'all

Beetlejuiced him."

Pulling up her message app, she read Max's text. She knew he was having a busy night with all of the partying around campus, but she smiled at the time he took to check on her. Quickly sending him a response, letting him know they were fine, she shoved the phone back in her waistband.

"Guys, is this the place where the party is supposed to be?" Astrid asked, stopping in front of a dark sketchy-looking house. Glancing around the neighborhood, Karlie realized they had wound up in the middle of a dark street in the middle of an even tougher area than where they lived.

"Hang on and I'll check the address," Sam said, pulling out her phone. After checking the text, she started typing a message. "It's the right place, but I texted my friend to see what he says. Maybe he got the address wrong."

"Hey, ladies, looking to party?" They spun around to see a large man leering at them from across the street. He looked like someone that belonged on this street, unlike them. Karlie could tell his eyes had a weird shiny quality in them in the little light the streetlights were putting off.

"Let's just go back," Astrid said quietly and they nodded in agreement. As they started back down the sidewalk, the man crossed the street to block their progress. Shoving Chiara behind her, Karlie quickly handed back her phone.

"Call Max," she whispered before moving her friends toward the other side of the street.

"Where you going, bitch? You too good to party with me?" The man was creeping closer to them as he spoke.

"Fuck off, asswipe," Sam sneered, turning to continue down the street.

Before Karlie knew what had happened, the man was standing right in front of her. He smelled of alcohol and looked slightly crazy. Karlie wished like anything Sam had just let her try to handle the situation.

She backed them up slowly away from him while looking

for anywhere they could escape to. The houses all looked dark in this area and there wasn't even one car parked on the street.

"What did you say to me, cunt?" the man asked Sam, even though he never took his eyes off of Karlie.

Just when she was afraid he was going to grab her, she heard a car squeal to a stop near them.

"Hey, buddy, is everything okay here?" Karlie felt a tear slide down her face as Max eased himself between them and the man. "How about we leave these girls alone. Where can I give you a ride to?"

Max held a hand out to the man, keeping him away from them as he backed them up behind him. Karlie felt Chiara grab her hand as they worked to back up the sidewalk.

"Fuck you, I was just talking to them. Those bitches need to learn some manners." The man spat at them.

"I hear you. Why don't we go across the street and talk about this?" In a flash, the man pulled a knife out of somewhere, aiming a slash at Max. "Fuck," he said, jumping back as the women screamed.

Before Karlie could count to one, Max had tackled him to the ground. She watched, clutched to her friends as they wrestled on the street, Max working to disarm him. Managing to wrap his legs around the man, Max pinned his back to his chest, locking one arm around his neck while pinning the knife to the ground with the other.

Max held on to the struggling man as more police cars arrived. With the help of two other officers, the man was relieved of his weapon before being spun onto his stomach as his hands were handcuffed behind his back.

Max spoke to one of the officers as his eyes locked on Karlie's over the top of the man's shoulder. The officers placed their attacker in the back of the squad car, then took their statement about what happened. With the man secured,

Max slowly walked over to them. He didn't take his eyes off of Karlie as he crossed the street.

"Are you okay?" he asked, checking her from head to toe before looking at her friends. Spying Chiara, he scowled for a moment before carefully reschooling his features.

"I-I think so," Karlie stammered out, wrapping her arms around herself as the adrenaline in her system was replaced by the reality of what had just happened. The man could have easily hurt or even killed one of them with that knife.

"I'm sorry," she whispered quietly, looking at Max's feet.

"Hey, look at me," he said, bringing her eyes to his. "That guy was high on something nasty. My guess is meth. I'm just glad the four of you are unhurt." He pulled her against him in a bear hug, adding Chiara when she let out a sob.

After Astrid and Sam made it a group hug, he eased them back so he could see everyone. "This is what you're going to do. I'm getting you a car to take you to Donnelly's. Get something to eat, have a soda," he added, emphasizing the word soda. "I'll come see you home as soon as I get off. Yeah?"

"You don't want us to go back to the apartment?" Karlie asked, refusing to let him go.

"I think you four look too good all dressed up to let some crackhead ruin your evening. Go hang out with your favorite bartender with the second-best ass in town." He smiled when they all laughed shakily.

Pulling out his phone, he ordered them a car to take them downtown. It was still a rowdy area, but with all the professionals that hung out down there, it was a much safer bet. When the car pulled up, he verified the driver before opening the doors.

"Thank you," Karlie told him when everyone else was loaded. Leaning against his Kevlar vest, she raised up on her tiptoes, brushing her lips over his cheek before ducking inside the car. Taking a deep breath, she waited as he paused before closing her door.

With two taps on the roof, he signaled for the driver to pull away. She gave a small wave. But, she was positive he couldn't see her as she stared out the back window at him standing in the street, watching them drive away.

————

Max was still standing in the middle of the street, trying to get his pulse to return to normal, when he heard someone jogging toward him. Spinning, he saw one of the other campus officers slow to a walk.

"Hey, is everything okay. I was trying to break up a fight at one of the apartments on this side of campus when I heard the call that you were in a knife fight."

Officer Pete Jackson was one of the other policemen on campus. Though he was a good twenty years older than Max, he was still in great shape. Max found that he liked the older man more than most of the other officers he worked with.

"How'd you get here?" Max asked, meeting the man at his SUV.

"Walked. Are you sure you're alright, you're bleeding." Looking at his arms, Max found a line of blood that had soaked through his left arm.

"Shit, he must have caught me with his blade."

"Come on, I'll drive you to the clinic to have that sewn up." Climbing into the driver's seat, Pete dropped Max off at the clinic before heading back to the office.

"You'll need to come fill out a report about that," he called out of the vehicle before driving off. With a sigh, Max walked into the clinic past kids barfing into buckets and holding ice on injuries.

After an hour of waiting for someone to sew his arm back up, then half an hour of filling out an incident report, he finally made it to his apartment to clean up. Quickly he ran through the shower before pulling on clean jeans and a button-down shirt.

Grabbing his jacket, he drove his motorcycle downtown, parking in back by Parker's Ram Charger. Walking around the front, he pushed through the front door of Donnelly's. Even through the crowd, he saw Karlie almost immediately.

"Hey, badass of the night, what would you like to drink? It's on the house." Parker waved him over to the bar. "The ladies have been regaling me with your exploits in wrestling would-be rapists and whatnot all evening." Max rolled his eyes at Parker as he motioned to the nearest tap.

Sliding the beer in front of him, Parker motioned toward the corner. "You'll find them in the corner minding their manners. In those outfits though, you might need to borrow my bat to keep the vultures at bay."

"Thanks, man." Max held up his beer in toast to the bartender before pushing through the crowd toward the back tables.

"Well, aren't you ladies every man's dream," he said, walking up to their table. They had been joined by one of their other flatmates, Emma he thought. She sat next to Astrid in a full Eeyore onesie.

Flinching from the sound of feminine squeals of greeting, he pulled Karlie up from her chair, reseating her on his lap when he sat down. He liked that the place was so packed she had to sit on his lap.

"You should be proud of us," Karlie said, snuggling against him. "We've turned down every offer of alcohol."

"We did go trick-or-treating down the street though. Parker said we would be safe if we stayed on this block. Look at the candy," Sam added, holding out a sack for him to see. "I think I have a sugar rush going."

"Actually, I think I'm done in for tonight. Anyone ready to call it quits?" Astrid asked with a yawn.

"Yeah, we'll head out with you. Max," Sam said, leaning

down to give him a peck on the cheek. "Thank you for coming to our rescue. Again."

She pulled Emma up with her, who then pulled Chiara to her feet. "Karlie, hope we don't see you again tonight. Ciao, babe." She gave a casual wave to Parker, who strode to the table to meet her. "Can you call us a ride, please?"

"Already done. I told my cousin to drop Catwoman off at her dorm first, then little Army, Eeyore and my wildest wet dream at the apartment." Parker held up a hand when Max started to speak. "He knows to watch until they are all safely inside. Don't worry, shade, I got this." He motioned them to follow him to the door.

With last calls of goodbye, they disappeared, leaving just Max with Karlie curled up on his lap.

"You want to find a spot at the bar for a while before I take you home?" Max asked as several patrons eyed their table.

"Sure," she answered as Max stood her back on her feet. Picking up her candy from the table, he took her hand to lead her to the only two empty spots at the bar.

Parker returned inside shortly, working down the bar, refilling drinks until he reached them.

"Hey, what's the name of the one in the cheerleader outfit?" he asked, leaning on the bar in front of them.

"Astrid?" Karlie said.

"Yeah, that's her. She's shy when she's sober, yeah?"

"She can be, but she's really fun. I didn't know her until she was assigned to our apartment. Astrid is actually a year older than us, so she's a junior this year." Parker nodded, listening until he was called to the other end of the bar.

"What do you think that's about?" she asked Max.

He had no idea, but he made a mental note to keep an eye on it. Parker seemed to be a decent enough guy, at least when Max had been around him in the past, but he ran with some rather shady characters. Astrid didn't need to get mixed up with whatever Parker had in mind.

"Are you about ready to go?" he asked, catching Karlie trying to stifle a yawn as he finished his beer. When she nodded, he helped her off the barstool, motioning for Parker to bring the bill.

"Sam picked up her and Karlie's bill. Yours was free, so have a good one. See you next time." Parker waved them off, crossing back to the other end of the bar. Walking out the door, they turned the corner to head to the back alley where the motorcycle was parked.

"Your legs are going to freeze," Max commented when they reached his bike. Karlie looked down at her legs. Even with her big coat on, she didn't have anything to protect them from the cold. Giving him her best sultry look, she fluttered her eyelashes.

"You'll just have to figure out how to keep me warm then." It was meant as a joke, but her laugh died in her throat when his dark eyes flashed to hers. He could think of a hundred ways he wanted to keep her warm at that instant, all of them turning his blood into fire.

"Kiss me, Max." Her words were so quiet, he was positive he wasn't meant to hear her. But that didn't stop him from crashing his mouth down onto hers. His insistence that she let him in as he flicked his tongue over the seam of her lips made her moan.

He plunged into her mouth, tasting every inch as their tongues danced. He ran one hand into her hair, angling her head so he could delve even deeper as the other gripped her hip, pulling her closer to him.

Fighting for control, his hand moved from her hip to her thigh, just under her skirt. Both of her hands were buried in his shirt as she tried to pull him closer, making him almost lose his mind. When he finally felt them both run out of air, he moved his hands to her waist, taking a step back as he broke the kiss.

"Thank you," Karlie said slowly, opening her eyes. Max

felt the deep rumbling of laughter slowly work its way out as a grin spread across his face.

"You're thanking me? No, no, the thanks is all mine," he said. "I'll never know what to expect, will I?"

"Is that a bad thing?" Karlie was still holding on to his shirt, looking up at him with those beautiful amber eyes. Max pulled her closer against him, wrapping his arms around her waist.

"I think it's the best thing. You're so beautiful, smart, and sweet, but I think the thing I love the most about you is how off balance you keep me. Every day, I can't wait to see what you'll throw at me.

"When Chiara called me this evening to tell me what was happening, it felt like my world stopped. All I could think about was getting to you." Max swallowed hard to keep his voice from wavering.

Reaching up, Karlie pulled him down to her lips again, sealing his fate. Nothing in this world would ever be as important to him as she was.

"I think I'm starting to freeze," she said, breaking the kiss.

"Shit, let's go. Do you need to get home or can I show you something?" Max asked, securing her helmet.

"Pretty sure after that kiss you can show me whatever you want," she answered with a wink. Shaking his head, he swung onto the motorcycle, pulling her tight up against his back as he drove out of the alley.

CHAPTER
Eight

"MAX, THIS IS AMAZING!" Karlie said, looking over her shoulder at him from his apartment's bathroom doorway. Seeing him visibly relax, she wondered if he had been nervous about bringing her here.

"I still need to buy some more furniture, but everything's been painted. Luckily, the floors were in good shape."

Looking around, she took in his apartment. It was small but comfortable with one bedroom and bathroom, a living area with room between his couch and open kitchen for a table, and a nice television on one wall.

Walking into the kitchen area, Karlie ran her fingertips over the appliances. They were older models, but a good size and extremely clean.

"I think it's perfect just the way it is." She moved into the living area, taking in the blanket folded on the back of the couch. "When did you decide to move out of your mom's?"

"Actually, I was kicked out the night you came over after the stove exploded." She kicked off her shoes, sitting down to watch him put a pan on the stove.

When he had their hot chocolate ready, he carried two mugs over to the couch. "So what you're saying is, your mom kicked you out because of me?" she asked, raising an eyebrow in question as she took a sip from her mug. "That makes me a femme fatale. Mmm, I like that idea."

He laughed, trying not to spill his drink. "In that outfit, you look more like a vice sting," he laughed. "Where were you going tonight?"

"We went to Lauren's for a party but Sam heard about another one down the street. Only when we got there, no one was around." Karlie couldn't stop the shiver that raced up her body at the thought of what could have happened if Max hadn't arrived. "We were just heading back when that guy started yelling at us. I can't believe you tackled him."

"Yeah, the fucker cut my arm. I'm pretty sure he was tweaking on something nasty."

Slowly, Karlie set her mug down on the floor next to the couch. She couldn't believe their stupidity had gotten Max hurt. Taking the mug out of his hand, she added it to hers before standing up in front of him.

"Show me," she whispered.

"It's not a big deal, just a couple of stitches on my arm. Not even bad enough to miss work," he said, looking up at her with a smile.

Reaching down, Karlie slowly pulled his shirt off over his head. Kneeling in front of him, she ran her fingers across the skin next to the cut before following it with gentle kisses.

"I'm so sorry I got you hurt," she said, meeting his eyes. She watched as they turned from their deep brown to almost black as he stared down at her. Suddenly, he reached up, pulling her onto his lap to straddle his legs.

"It's not your fault," he said. "It's the fucker's who thought he could mess with you." Running his hand into her hair, he pulled her to him, searing her through when their lips met. She wondered if every time he kissed her, it would set her on fire.

When his tongue slid between her lips, she decided she

could give just as good as she was getting. Within moments, their kiss reached a carnal level even more intense than the last one. He ground up against her heat when she nipped at his bottom lip. She had no doubt he wanted her based on the rock-hard erection growing beneath her.

Before she could act on it, though, he pulled back, stopping her hips with his strong hands.

"What's wrong?" Karlie asked.

"We should probably slow down before you make me come in my jeans. I didn't ask you over to jump you." She sat looking at him for a moment while she pondered that thought over. Does it count if she jumped him instead? Admittedly, the jeans were a little uncomfortable to grind against and she assumed they had to be cutting off his blood flow by now.

"Okay." Reaching between them, she unhooked his jeans, running the zipper down until they were open.

"Karlie," Max started to say. He said he liked being thrown off his game, well get ready mister.

"Stop talking and lift your hips." Max clamped his mouth shut, lifting just enough she could wiggle his jeans past his knees. Leaving his boxer briefs in place, she looked down. The man was huge.

"What?" he asked, looking down at where she was staring.

"We're leaving the underwear on for now. That thing looks a little intimidating." Max started to laugh until she lowered herself, sliding her heat up his length. That's when the laugh turned into a string of moaned curses. It felt so good as she rocked her hips against him.

"Hold on," she said, getting off him. She tried not to laugh at his look of desperation. Quickly she unhooked her skirt, letting it fall to the floor before pulling her shirt off over her head. Straddling his lap again, she made a test run up him. "That's much better."

"Fuck, yeah it is." Pulling her toward him, Karlie

gasped when Max nipped at her hard nub through her bra. She had chosen to wear her best black set for no other reason than it made her outfit complete in her eyes. Now she was glad she did, since it seemed to make him even harder.

With a quick flick of his fingers at her back, he had her bra undone, pulling it off her body. When he bent his head, this time sucking her nipple between his lips as he moved her up and down his shaft, she almost lost her mind.

"Max," she moaned as heat started to build at her core, spiraling through her body. "Max, don't stop." She barely recognized her own shaky voice; it had grown so hoarse with desire.

With help from him, she slid her panties down her legs so he now rubbed directly on her clit. Even through his briefs, she could feel him straining as he ground up at her. His mouth was on her neck, nibbling up the side until it gently pulled her earlobe inside.

"You need to come, Karlie," he whispered in her ear. She felt herself spiral apart in his arms as he continued to whisper in her ear, pulling her tight to him.

When she finally regained her senses, she found herself plastered against his heaving chest as their hearts raced together. He kissed her temple as she lay in his arms. Never before had she felt so happy in the moment as she did right now with Max.

"Did you finish?" she said, suddenly worried about him. She heard him chuckle softly.

"Yeah, but you might need a shower. When do you have practice tomorrow?"

"In the afternoon. I need to be in the gym around three."

"Good. You can stay here tonight."

"Well, since it's already after midnight, that's probably a good idea." She stayed in his arms a few more minutes until she shivered from the cold.

"I'm heading for the shower," she said, sitting back up on his thighs.

"Okay. Sorry about the mess," Max said, helping her off his legs.

"Why? This is the first time I've done this. You are so much better at this orgasm thing that I am by myself even if it is a little messy." Gathering up her clothes, she walked toward the bathroom.

"Thanks?" she heard from the living room. Shooting a smile over her shoulder, she stepped into the bathroom, closing the door.

When she finally emerged from the shower, she found Max pulling a T-shirt out of his dresser for her. Turning around, he froze as she walked toward him in her towel.

"Everything okay?" she asked when she stopped in front of him. "This mine?" Reaching out, she tried to pry the T-shirt out of his hands, but he held on tight. With a tug, he pulled the towel off from around her. "Max!"

"You're so beautiful," he said as he let his eyes wander down her body. Turning bright red, she snatched at the T-shirt once again. This time, he opened his fist, letting her have it.

"I'm going to run through the shower, then I'll be back," he said, shaking his head.

Karlie slid between the covers after pulling the shirt over her head. It was one of his police academy shirts that hit her midthigh. She had almost fallen asleep when she felt the bed dip behind her.

Scooting back on the bed into his arms, she sighed, drifting off when he wrapped himself around her. It was the perfect ending to an exciting day.

––––––––

Max sat on the bed studying a sleeping Karlie. She was sprawled in the bed on her stomach with her arms above her pillow. The covers had been kicked off and the T-shirt he gave her rode to just below her ass cheeks. Was he allowed to roll her over on her back to make breakfast out of her?

Looking at the clock, he frowned, seeing it was only seven in the morning. Would she be pissed about the early hour or him between her legs more? He had no fucking clue.

She had made it clear last night that she wasn't ready for straight sex, but was oral sex off-limits as well? She hadn't had any problem riding him last night with nothing but his boxer briefs between them.

While he was still contemplating what to do, she flipped over in the bed, flinging her arms back up over her head, exposing her body to him. With a smile, he tilted his head to the side, studying her. This must be a sign from God.

Lying down next to her, he slowly eased his hand under her shirt, cupping her breast. Arching slightly with a moan, he took that as another sign, tweaking her nipple into a hard point.

Working her shirt up above her breast, he leaned down, pulling her nipple into his mouth. Fuck, she was perfect. Her breast fit in his hand like it was made for it. Raising up on his forearms, he pushed her legs apart, settling between them so he could pay more attention to her other breast.

"Max," she moaned, rocking her hips against him. Releasing her nipple, he worked his way down her body, placing gentle kisses as he went. "Max, what are you doing?" When he reached her thighs, he pushed them open. Settling his shoulders between her thighs, he wrapped his arms under her.

"Oh, god," she moaned at his first lick through her folds. She got louder when he lightly sucked her clit between his lips before running his tongue back down to her entrance.

He decided having his own apartment had been a brilliant idea when she grabbed his hair, pulling him back up to her clit. With a cry, he felt her lose herself a few minutes later.

With his long arms, he reached up, rolling her nipples between his strong fingers as he continued to work her body. She rolled straight into another orgasm as he felt himself follow her over.

He leveled up slightly, resting his head on her stomach as she ran her hand through his hair. There was nowhere else he wanted to be right now except here. Well, he wouldn't mind being inside her, but this was a damn good second.

"Good morning," he said, sitting up on his knees.

"Good morning," she answered with a stretch. "Holy fuckbuckets."

"I'm not sure if that's good or bad," he said, his eyebrows knitting in confusion.

"That's better than good. Did you know there are around eight thousand nerves in the clitoris? I think you hit them all. Thank you." Max laughed, a deep rumble. Only Karlie would know that fact.

Leaning down, he gave her a quick kiss before climbing off her.

"I have to go clean up, then wash the sheets," he smirked.

"Sorry. Is this something to look forward to every time we mess around?"

"Probably. I can't 'mess around' with you and not come, especially with my face between your legs." He watched as the red crept up her neck before she smiled at him.

"Then I'll make breakfast while you take care of Mad Max." Hopping off the bed, she pulled her T-shirt back down.

"Mad Max?" he asked, walking toward the bathroom.

"I figured it needs a name. I don't think that's it, but I'll keep working on it." She laughed at his scowl.

"You're crazy. You know that, right?"

"Yes," she said, pulling on a pair of his sweatpants. Walking past him, she placed a chaste kiss on the corner of his mouth. "But you know you love me," she said in jest, smacking his ass when he turned to enter the bathroom. He yelped some noise he hadn't made since puberty, closing the door quickly behind him.

Max knew her comment was meant to be funny, but the thing was, he really did think he loved her. His life hadn't been the same since she opened the door to that crappy apartment. He had been amused by the way she had looked him over, but that hadn't explained why he continued to pursue her.

They still had obstacles in the way, though, and he hated that it felt like they had to sneak around. He wondered how much longer they could keep up their charade on campus before one of them made a slip. Tomorrow, when he saw her, he would have to act like she was just a casual acquaintance. After last night, he knew that would be next to impossible.

After taking a quick shower, Max pulled on a pair of sweatpants before wandering into the kitchen. Karlie had her earbuds in, dancing with her back to him in front of the stove. Leaning against the wall, he watched as she sang, pouring batter into the skillet. Somehow his world had become blissfully domestic.

Easing up behind her, he wrapped his long arms around her waist, pulling her against him. Taking the earbuds out of her ears, she laid them on the counter as she snuggled against his chest, watching breakfast cook.

"What are we having?" he asked, looking around her.

"It's the weekend. The answer will always be pancakes, unless it's waffles. Weekdays are usually egg sandwiches, but the weekend is special. It requires syrup and bacon. Oh, I can make French toast as well." She flipped the pancakes over as he hid his grin in her hair.

"Did you know that French toast was originally called lost bread in France because they used the leftover bread instead of throwing it out?" That random fact made him grin even bigger.

"Is that so?" he asked.

"You can make bread pudding or Thanksgiving dressing the same way." Max felt Karlie suddenly grow stiff against him. "Are you making fun of me?" she asked.

Turning her in his arms, he took the spatula out of her hands, setting it down before wrapping his hands around her waist to lift her onto the counter next to it.

"I would never make fun of you. It just amazes me how many random facts you know off the top of your head," he said, looking into her eyes.

"It is ridiculous, isn't it? I'll try to stop."

"If you do, I will torture you until you start again." Max narrowed his eyes, plastering a wicked grin across his face as he pulled her against him.

Leaning down, he ran his hands into her hair, kissing her for everything he was worth. When she moaned, he devoured her until the smell of smoke made them break apart.

"Max, the pancakes!" Karlie said, pushing him back to jump off the counter.

"I'll eat those," he volunteered as she pulled the well-done pancakes out of the skillet.

"You're not eating the first thing I've made you in your new apartment burned," she answered. "Go sit at the table while I make another batch."

Max walked to the table, taking a seat on the opposite side of where Karlie was pulling ingredients out of the refrigerator. Even the smell of burned pancakes couldn't diminish his smile. He had to stop himself from laughing at Karlie muttering under her breath.

"Getting me all distracted so I burn the pancakes. This isn't a game, Officer Scaletti."

"Call me Officer Scaletti again and I'll handcuff you to the bed," Max growled at her.

"Will you place my hands on the table, kick my legs apart and search for contraband first?" she asked with a laugh, bringing the orange juice over to the table.

"Can you not let me eat at least one meal without a hard-on the entire time?" She laughed harder, walking back to the stove to flip the next batch of pancakes. When they were ready, she plated up a stack on each plate, adding bacon.

Max dug in like he hadn't eaten in ages. He had heard stories from her roommates that she was as good a cook as his mother, but other than lunch, he hadn't had a chance to eat much of it. If his luck held, it would be the first of many meals they shared.

CHAPTER

Nine

"I'M GOING to need any and all details of the after-party last night. Who won the pool?" Sam asked, sticking her head into the kitchen as Karlie put together a quick snack.

Max had dropped her off earlier to give her plenty of time to get ready for practice. The conference tournament started this week, so she needed to make sure her head was in the game.

"No one won. There's been no sex," she replied, drawing an eye roll from Sam.

"Well, that's disappointing. You mean after saving us from near death, you didn't throw that poor man a bone?"

"I didn't say nothing happened, I said there was no sex. So if anyone asks, there is nothing going on." With a wink, Karlie walked past Sam to grab her bag from her room.

Sam followed her, shaking her head. "I don't know how you keep your hands off of something that fine."

"Who says I do?" With a final smirk at her best friend, Karlie swung her bag over her shoulder, taking the steps two at a time.

By the time she walked to the gym, she had just enough time to change her shoes before warming up. Putting Max out of her mind, she began running through the defensive drills that, though boring, would be essential to winning.

By Tuesday evening, the team was ready to begin the first game of the tournament. It was one of the better conferences in New England, so Karlie knew their opponent wouldn't go down without a fight.

Waiting for the down ref to check the starting rotation, she caught a glimpse of Max in his uniform standing by the door. With a smile, she gave him a chin lift before heading onto the court to replace one of the middle blockers on the back row.

When they finally pulled out the win in the fifth set, Karlie looked around for Max. He had left sometime during her game on a call she guessted. Turning back to the stands, she was greeted by her friends congratulating her on the win.

After cleaning up, she joined them for some much-needed carbs at their favorite Italian place. Well, actually, it was her second favorite now. She had to quell her disappointment when Max didn't sweep in to rescue his sister from financial embarrassment again.

Before she knew it, the week had flown by, landing the team in the conference finals. Between her classes, practice, and Max's work schedule, they had only been able to see each other in passing.

With a sigh, she found herself packing her bag in her room for the bus that left in an hour. Sam was sitting quietly in the beanbag watching as Gemma ignored them with her headphones on at her desk.

Shoving her volleyball shoes in the bottom of the bag, she heard her phone vibrate.

Max: When do you leave?

Karlie: In an hour.

Max: You'll be great.

Karlie: I wish you could tell me that in person.

Max: Then come to the back door.

With a grin, Karlie zipped up her bag, leaving it on the

bed as she rushed out of her room. Without answering Sam who was yelling after her, she raced through the apartment.

Wiggling past the half-open door that was partially blocked by their table still, she flew down the stairs, jerking the door open at the bottom. Finding Max standing at the bottom of the steps, she jumped into his arms, pulling him in for a kiss.

It was obvious that he was still at work since she was wrestling around that damn Kevlar, trying to pull him closer. When she finally ran out of air, Max set her back on the step. Taking a step back, he ran his hand through his hair, looking at her.

"I don't think I'll ever get tired of that," he said with a grin.

"Let's hope not. Do you know it's illegal, according to some old law, for men to kiss their wives in Hartford, Connecticut, on Sundays?"

"Thank God we don't live in Hartford then," Max answered with a chuckle.

"I have to go."

"I know. Go play your game, baby. You're going to obliterate them."

Looping his hand around her neck, Max pulled her forward for one more quick kiss before turning her toward the door.

"Oh crap, I locked myself out." With a shake of his head, he reached around her with his master key to open the door. "Bye, Max," she said with one last look before running back up the stairs.

"Bye, Karlie."

Jogging toward her teammates, she barely made it when the bus pulled up. They had agreed to pick them up next to the gym this time. Piling onto the small bus, Karlie found her seat next to the setter near the back. As the bus pulled out for its hour trip where the finals would be held, she caught a glimpse of a tall, dark-haired policeman watching it leave.

Max looked at his watch for the tenth time in the last half hour. If everything held to plan, he would be out of here in fifteen minutes. He could be changed and ready to go when Chiara arrived. She had expressed a desire to go to the city to watch the game, so Max had quickly agreed to take her.

The school had chartered a fan bus for those wishing to see the finals to ride on, but he didn't want to be trapped on a bus full of kids for that long.

It was always a perilous ride to take the motorcycle down the interstate, but it wouldn't be the first time they had done it and lived to tell about it. With any luck, traffic wouldn't be bad tonight.

Finally it was time for him to clock out. Quickly changing into his street clothes, he was met by his sister walking out of the office.

"Do you think we'll make it in time to see the first serve?" Chiara asked, jogging next to him to keep up with his long strides.

"We'll be close."

Reaching his motorcycle, he unlocked their helmets, giving Chiara the extra one. Swinging on to his bike, he quickly started it, pulling out of the parking lot the second his sister settled behind him. She was wearing a backpack on her back that she had shoved a change of clothes in.

Max had made arrangements for them to stay with a cousin in the city so they could see the championship game in the morning if Karlie's team won tonight. The trip into the city was cold, but fortunately they still hadn't received any early snow yet.

Pulling up to the gym, Max parked his bike, locking up

their helmets. Walking into the stands, he was amazed to see how many people had come to support the team.

"Come on, I see Sam. We can sit with her." Grabbing him by the hand, Chiara pulled Max behind her until they plopped down next to Karlie's best friend.

"Hey, Karlie didn't tell me you were coming," she said, looking over at him.

"We weren't sure Max would get off in time," Chiara answered for him.

"From what I heard, it sounds like he almost got off earlier this afternoon." Max opened his mouth to respond to Sam's comment when the crowd stood around him with a cheer.

Standing, he saw the team take their positions on the court with Karlie standing on the side, waiting to substitute in for the middle. Watching her scan the crowd, he grinned when her face lit up, finding him. She gave him a tiny wave before slapping hands with the girl she was replacing on the court as she ran by.

"Can you be any more obvious?" Chiara asked, elbowing him in the ribs.

"Remember, this place is filled with staff, which also includes the dean of students sitting down two rows," Sam added. Max surveyed the crowd, picking out several members of the administration before turning back to Sam.

"I'll remember." With a nod, she turned back to watch the first serve.

The team was revved up to a fevered pitch, only taking four sets to win. They would be returning tomorrow to play in the championship game at nine in the morning.

After telling Sam good night, they climbed out of the stands to wish Karlie congratulations. Max was careful to always keep Chiara between them so no one got the wrong impression.

"I can't believe you came," Karlie said, looking past Chi. "Will you be here tomorrow?"

"We wouldn't miss it," he replied, wishing he could pull her to him. "We're crashing at a cousin's here in the city."

"Ms. James, fantastic game," the dean of students said, walking up behind them. With a nod, Max pulled Chiara with him toward the door. Of all the people on campus, he would be the worst possible person to find out about them.

In the parking lot, he handed his sister her helmet, waiting to strap his on until he saw Karlie leave the gym. With one more longing glance at him, she stepped onto the bus.

Only after the bus turned out of sight did Max start the motorcycle.

Driving across the city, they pulled into the parking lot outside his cousin's apartment. It had been a while since either of them had seen her, so Max was looking forward to catching up. They spent the evening visiting before turning in for the night.

He rousted his sister out of the guest bed early the next morning so they could grab breakfast before returning to the gym.

Finding the gym already packed, Max was grateful that Sam had managed to save them seats in the top of the stands. The team was already on the court warming up so he quickly scanned the floor until he spotted her.

Karlie had on what Max had come to know as her game face. He knew soon she would block out everything but the game. The crowd would disappear from around her, the noise would fade as she focused just on those of her teammates, even the pain of the hard dives to the floor would barely register.

"If you don't relax, you're never going to make it through the game," Sam said, smirking at him. He scowled at her until she rolled her eyes. She was right, though, he was a nervous wreck.

He had spent a couple of years boxing for the police's team, but watching someone else compete, someone he cared about, was much worse than actually playing himself. Max suffered through the national anthem, starting players' names and opening huddle with a monster knot in his stomach.

"She's right," Chiara said next to him. "There's nothing you can do to help her. This will be the hardest game they've played this year. They lost to this team in the regular season." He didn't know if Chiara was trying to help or send him into cardiac arrest.

"It's fine, she's fine," he mumbled as he watched Karlie receive the first serve, perfectly placing it in the setter's hands.

"There you go, Ponch. Just keep up the mantra." Sam just laughed at the scowl he gave her this time as they sat down.

"Ponch? You had to go all the way back to *CHIPS* to come up with something?"

"Seemed appropriate." He ignored his sister, who snorted a laugh.

"Erik Estrada?"

"Naturally."

He sat for a moment, feeling the knot slowly untwist from his guts. Fighting the need to grin, he finally shrugged, returning his focus to the game.

"Not going to lie, I don't hate it."

Sam laughed, shaking her head. "Careful, officer, Karlie is starting to erode your grouchy exterior." Max smirked at Sam. He was starting to see why she had become Karlie's best friend.

Scowling at the giggling next to him, he shoved his shoulder against his sister, making her bump into Sam. "What are you giggling at?"

Turning back to the game, he chose to ignore them until the end of the first set. Even though it was a close game, the other team won. Max wasn't too worried, he had learned over the season that Karlie's team didn't always hit its stride until after the first set.

Changing sides, they waited for the down ref to check the rotation before Karlie walked to the back of the court. When the whistle blew, Max watched her throw the ball in the air before jumping over the back line to hit it into a seam on the other side, earning a serving ace.

He couldn't help but cheer with everyone. His girl had a hell of an arm on her.

Her team rallied in the second set, winning it by the required two points in the end. Splitting the next two sets, the championship finally came down to the fifth set. Since it was only played to fifteen instead of the regular twenty-five of the other sets, Karlie's team had to start out strong.

Winning the coin flip, her team opted to serve first. Walking to the back of the court, she didn't run to serve the ball this time. Instead, she tossed it above her head, hitting it slightly in front of herself, making the ball wobble in the air. When it dropped just behind the front row, making their libero dive to the ground just short, the crowd roared.

By the time they traded court sides after eight points, the crowd was on its feet. Karlie's team only trailed the defending champions by one point.

Max watched as Karlie bent at the waist, getting in position. With her hands, she motioned for the server to send her the ball while yelling at her other defensive players. He would never understand how he found that angry warrior face such a turn-on, but he knew he would desperately love to push her against the mats at the back of the court and show her how much he liked it.

Rising to her invitation, the server sent the ball straight at her. Karlie shot forward, bumping the ball into the air above her setter's hands without even leaving her feet. When the outside hitter sent the ball in a blur to the floor just inside the back line, the noise in the gym rose.

Feeding off the energy, Karlie yelled even louder at the defense, pointing out what seams they needed to cover, who would go short, who had free balls. Max grinned, knowing the free balls were always picked up by her and pity the player that got in her way.

As the last kill was registered by Karlie's team, the team went crazy. They had defeated the returning champions by two points. Max jumped up and down with the rest of the fans in the stands, hugging first his sister, then Sam.

They watched as the team's coach received the trophy, eliciting even more screaming from the team members. Max had never seen so many women crying at one time, not even at a wake, but he guessed this was worth a tear or two.

When the medal ceremony was over, with Karlie picking up defensive player of the tournament, he followed Chiara out of the stands. Pulling away from all of the celebrating fans on the court, he found a spot he could wait near the wall.

Sam and his sister had melded into the crowd to find Karlie, but he knew his congratulations would need to wait until later. Now even the president of the university was here, watching.

Max was standing with his hands in his pockets waiting patiently when he heard his name screamed. Looking up, he saw Karlie running toward him. Tears of joy were rolling down her face, but her grin lit up her whole face. It was the most beautiful thing he had ever seen.

As if in slow motion, she launched herself at him, crashing their mouths together as he caught her. He felt his back hit the wall hard, but he managed to hang on.

"We did it, Max. We won. We're going to the tournament." Karlie was still wrapped around him when she let him come up for air. She had explained to him earlier that the winner of the conference tournament got an automatic bid to the NCAA tournament.

"I know, baby. You were amazing." His heart was hammering in his chest. He knew who was here and what her actions would mean to them both. But he refused to take away any of her happiness in this moment. He would sort out the repercussions later.

With one more kiss, she let her legs drop from around his waist, sliding back to the floor.

"I've got to go. See you at school tomorrow?" She waved with a grin before running back over to her team for pictures.

"I'll expect you in my office at nine tomorrow morning. You're to have no other contact with her until then. Do I make myself clear?" Max looked up to find the dean of students standing next to the university president.

"Yes, sir," he answered. Max slumped against the wall when they turned to walk away. Bending over, he placed his hands on his knees.

He knew this would happen if he continued to see her, but it had knocked him on his ass anyway. They would fire him for sure from the police department, he just worried what would happen to Karlie. His mind started to run through a myriad of ideas to protect her.

"Max, are you okay?" He heard Chiara ask, standing in front of him. Straightening, he met the worry in her eyes with the same stoic expression that had served him for years.

"Yeah, we need to go."

Turning, he stalked toward the door, assuming she would follow. When they got to the parking lot, she grabbed his sleeve, spinning him around to look at her.

"No, it's not. What happened?"

Pulling out of her grip, he continued toward his motorcycle, listening as Chiara jogged behind him, trying to catch up. Handing her the spare helmet, he swung onto the seat, starting the bike up.

When she had settled behind him, he quickly pulled away from the gym toward the interstate to take them home. The sooner he got home, the sooner he could figure out what his next steps would be.

CHAPTER
Ten

THE REST of the day proceeded like a dream. Karlie's team went out to lunch to celebrate, followed by a boisterous trip back to campus. Sam insisted she clean up so they could go out again for dinner.

Everywhere she went, people talked excitedly about their win. It seemed like their entire side of town was celebrating along with the team. Knowing how significant the campus was to this community, Karlie wasn't really surprised, though.

By the time she dropped into her beanbag that night to catch up on some homework due the next day, she was exhausted.

"Hey," Sam said, walking into the room holding her phone. "Have you heard from Max? Chiara just text saying he was acting really freaked about something but he wouldn't talk about it."

"No. As a matter of fact, it's odd for him not to make sure I made it back okay. Hang on." Grabbing her phone, Karlie quickly typed out a text to Max.

Karlie: Hey. Everything okay?
Max: Yeah. Great job today.

Karlie: Thanks. Chiara said you were acting funny.

Max: Chiara should learn to mind her own business.

Karlie: Wow! I can feel the claws from here.

Max: Sorry. Just tired.

Karlie: I'm really glad you came today.

Max: Promise me that whatever happens, you'll remember I think you're amazing.

Karlie: Max, what's going on?

Max: Promise me, Karlie.

Karlie: I promise. You're starting to worry me.

Max: Good night, beautiful.

Karlie: Good night, Max.

"That was weird. Chiara's right, something is going on. He says he's just tired." Karlie looked at Sam with concern, knitting her eyebrows. "I'll catch him tomorrow." With a shrug, Sam walked back out of the room.

Sliding her earbuds back in her ears, Karlie felt she had missed something important. Whatever it was floated on the periphery of her mind, not quite forming. Trying to focus on her work, she put whatever it was out of her mind.

The next morning, Karlie woke to an email from the dean of students requesting that she come by his office at her earliest convenience. That was never a good sign.

Crawling out of bed, she checked her day planner to see when she had time. Between classes and practice, she found half an hour in the afternoon. Responding to the email with her available time, she quickly dressed, grabbed breakfast, and headed out the door.

Fortunately, her first class was with Mr. Simms, the attorney who taught the law class. The hour passed quickly and soon, Karlie was running for practice. She knew this week would be tough as they prepared for the first round of the tournament.

By lunch, she was already exhausted. Taking a seat at their picnic table, Karlie pulled out her lunch, spreading it out in front of her. Looking around, she hunted for Max. They hadn't talked about meeting today, but she thought he might wander by anyway.

When she finished, having not seen any sign of him, she checked her watch, seeing she needed to head toward the dean's office. Come to think of it, she hadn't seen Max on campus at all today.

"Have a seat, Ms. James. He'll be free in a moment," the receptionist said, pointing to one of the chairs when she walked in. Sliding into a chair near the wall, she waited with a sense of dread. Whatever it was she couldn't quite bring to the front of her mind continued to nag at her. She pulled up her reading app on her phone to finish the fantasy she had started on the bus over the weekend.

"Ms. James, if you could join us, please." The dean's voice from his door made her jump. What did he mean by "us"? Grabbing her backpack, she followed him into his office.

"Please take a seat. I asked Mrs. Rodman and Officer Rogers to join us." She nodded at them, feeling her anxiety amp up. "It's come to our attention that one of the campus police officers has become an issue where you are concerned." Karlie felt herself dropping slowly into the seat that he had pointed to.

"You were seen at the tournament this weekend kissing Officer Scaletti." Oh god, she hadn't even thought about it. She felt her hands start to shake, so she clamped them in front of her in her lap.

"He was dismissed this morning for breaking campus policy. Normally, we would suspend you, but he laid out a strong argument this morning to simply have you placed on probation." He had been fired because of her and he knew last night what would happen. She tried to listen to what the counselor was telling her, but it was hard over the buzzing in her ears.

"Would you like to press charges for anything that might

have happened?" the head of university police asked. "You have a case for a sexual harassment charge at the very least."

"No," she answered, shaking her head.

"I'll go back to my office then," he said, standing. "Ms. James, I'm sorry we didn't act on the rumors that have been circulating about him. We should have done a better job protecting you." With a nod, he walked out the door, closing it again behind him. What did they think Max had done to her?

Before she could open her mouth to set the record straight, the dean continued. "You'll be allowed to play in the tournament, but you will report to Mrs. Rodman twice a week for counseling and a reprimand will be put in your file.

"If you get approached by any other members of the staff without reporting it immediately, you will be subject to expulsion. We take this very seriously, Ms. James. You may go if there is nothing else you would like to add."

Taking her bag, Karlie stood up, turning on legs that moved her out of his office through sheer will. She made it to the bottom of the steps of the administration building before the tears started streaming.

Running into the first bathroom she came to, Karlie locked herself in a stall. Taking several deep breaths, she fought to make sense of what had happened. In a nutshell, with one moment of blind celebration she had gotten Max fired and herself put on probation.

She really needed to talk to someone. Unfortunately, the one person she wanted to talk to more than anyone was probably so pissed at her he wouldn't take her call. Not that she had time to find out, she had to be in class for a test in five minutes.

Leaving the stall, she splashed water on her face, taking in her puffy eyes. Great, now she looked as bad as she felt. With any luck, no one would notice her anyway.

Of course, luck never had a way of appearing when you

truly needed it. Her class was just as excited to talk about their win as the one earlier had been. The only difference was, before Karlie had been excited to share the details. Now she just saw the look she had missed then on Max's face.

When she thought about it, he had looked both shocked and resigned after she kissed him. Why wasn't she smart enough to realize the crowd in the gym had included several of the administration?

It was a huge relief when the professor called everyone to attention before handing out the quiz. She struggled, trying to focus on the dates needed on the history of the Middle Ages test.

Praying she had at least pulled a B on the test, she headed out of the classroom. She had to meet her team back at the gym for pictures promoting their trip to the NCAA tournament. Pulling back on her uniform, she smiled for the pictures, wishing she could still feel as excited about it as she had only this morning.

Leaving the gym, she headed inside the library to meet about a project in marketing with the other three members assigned. They worked until time for dinner to come up with a new branding concept for one of the major retailers they had been given.

By the time Karlie climbed the steps to her room, it was all she could do to move. She hadn't received even one text from Max all day.

Finding her luck still avoiding her, she greeted her roommate, receiving a steely glare in return. The one night she could really use some time alone, Gemma was fully ensconced on her bed. Judging by her reaction, Karlie had an evening of passivity to enjoy.

Throwing her backpack on her bed, she headed to the kitchen only to find someone had eaten the leftover mac and cheese she had saved, knowing she would be too tired to cook tonight.

"Fuck it," she said, pulling out the peanut butter as she pressed the speed dial for Max. When the call went right to voice mail, she debated for a moment between sobbing and screaming. The scream won the argument.

"Shit," Sam said, walking into the kitchen. "I swear your roommate ate your food." She held up both hands, palms out in surrender.

"Of course she did," Karlie growled, calling Max again with the same result. This time, she let it all go, throwing the peanut butter jar at the corner before roaring at the ceiling.

"Why do I feel like this is more than Gemma eating your food?" Sam asked, picking the peanut butter up where it had landed under the table. At least the jars are pretty sturdy, so Karlie didn't have to clean that up as well.

"Did you talk to Max?" Sam took a step back when Karlie spun around to skewer her with a glare.

"No, because I got him fired. I also got put on probation," she growled in frustration at her best friend seconds before the sobbing won out after all.

"Oh sweetie. What happened?" Sam asked, pulling Karlie into her arms. Sam held her tight until the tears lightened up. Pushing her gently into one of the kitchen chairs, Sam pulled the bread down to work on making them sandwiches.

"I kissed him. In front of half of the admin office at the championship game. I didn't even realize I had done it. I'm sure that's why Chiara was asking about why he was acting strange last night." Sam slid one of the sandwiches in front of Karlie as she sat down in front of her at the table.

"I'm so stupid. They asked if I wanted to file charges. I don't even know what for." Sam stood back up, grabbing two sodas out of the fridge before setting one in front of Karlie.

"Don't argue, one soda won't tank the game this weekend. Besides, it's one of Gemma's." Settling back in the chair, Sam took a bite of her sandwich, waiting for Karlie to finish speaking.

"He has to hate me for screwing everything up." She stared at her uneaten sandwich. Why had she even thought she was hungry?

"Have you talked to him?" Sam asked, pulling her eyes away from her sandwich.

"It goes straight to voice mail."

"He's probably just trying to figure this shit out," Sam added. Karlie felt her eyes growing watery again when Sam placed her hand on her arm. "I'll make a deal with you. If he doesn't call by the end of tomorrow, I'll stomp down to that cop shop myself and kick his ass." Sam smiled when Karlie gave her a wobbly laugh.

"Thanks, Sam."

"What are friends good for if it's not to kick their best friend's boyfriend's ass?" Karlie reached across the table, squeezing Sam's hand before sitting back in the chair.

Picking up her sandwich, she took a small bite. Soon Sam had her laughing at the latest campus gossip. Max would call her, she had to believe that. Anything else would crush her.

———

Max had had a hellish day. First, he was accused of sexual assault by the head of the university police, then he had been fired right before pleading to the dean to spare Karlie.

It had helped win his case when he pointed out there wasn't a good backup libero on the team. If he suspended her, he would not only punish the entire team but ruin the volleyball team's first tournament bid in the school's history. He had stayed up doing his homework last night to build a case against her suspension.

After cleaning out his locker while the other guys watched, he was escorted off campus by Pete Jackson, the one guy he had really learned to respect.

He had been told to report directly to Lieutenant Mason

the second he walked into police headquarters, where he was treated to ten minutes of silence while he stood in front of his desk. The dress down he received afterward hadn't been much better. At least he still had a job as a cop in the end.

When he was released from in front of his lieutenant's desk, it was to be sent to the gym to work out. Arriving, he found he had to do not only the regular workout, but had to stay for the SWAT one as well.

He was pretty sure they were going to just kill him instead of letting him go. He had just closed his eyes, slumped on one of the benches in the locker room when a couple of the patrol officers walked in.

"Hey, Scaletti. Heard you got caught nutting one of the coeds," one of the guys said as he walked past. "I guess you've moved up from gang pussy." Max opened his eyes, scowling at the man.

"No. Don't talk about her," he warned with a shake of his finger.

"Why? Not got enough of that rich teenage cunt yet?" The men laughed until Max grabbed the man who had spoken by the front of his shirt, pulling him within a couple inches of his face.

"Say one more word, motherfucker," he growled at the man.

"Scaletti!" he heard barked behind him, followed by the other men coming to attention. Closing his eyes for a moment, he finally pushed the man against the lockers, releasing him. He could not catch a fucking break today. Turning, he came to attention as his lieutenant walked toward him.

"You men have somewhere better to be?" With a mumbled 'yes, sir', they quickly gathered up their stuff while Lieutenant Mason continued to stare at Max. "Put your uniform on. You can go do foot patrol in the park until you cool off."

"Yes, sir." Max waited until his boss was gone before he sat back down on the bench. Taking a deep breath, he spun around to face his locker, stripping off his T-shirt.

When he had fully changed into his uniform, he headed to the big park that mostly boasted dealers and prostitutes this time of the night. It was two in the morning before he was allowed to go home.

Checking his phone when he finally got home, he groaned at the number of times he had missed Karlie's calls. He was exhausted and had to be back to work in the morning to work out again, but he couldn't let her think he had just ignored her.

He sat down on the bed, pushing her speed dial number. Max decided he could at least leave her a message.

"Hello," she whispered. It took him a moment to recognize that she had actually answered the phone.

"Hey. Why are you awake?" He listened to a door open and close before she responded.

"Why are you awake?" she asked. Fair question.

"They're trying to kill me at work. What did the dean say?"

"Max, I'm so sorry. I don't know what I was thinking."

"You were excited and wanted to share it with your boyfriend. Now what did the dean say?"

"I'm on probation. A letter was placed in my file and I have to meet with a counselor. They asked if I wanted to file charges." Max was silent as he tried to remember to breathe. He hadn't even thought about them throwing the suggestion of filing charges against him to her. "Max?"

"I'm here. Listen, I don't think we should see each other for a while. I don't want you to get into any more trouble." He closed his eyes, hearing a sniffle in the phone. "I just...I just don't want to ruin your college career." His heart felt like it was being wrenched from his body as he listened to her cry quietly. "Okay?"

"Okay," she said, barely above a whisper. "Goodbye, Max."

"Goodbye, beautiful," he answered to dead air after she hung up.

With a roar, he threw his phone against the wall before falling back onto his bed. He had kept telling himself that it would be worth getting caught to see her, but nothing was worth hearing her cry as she said goodbye.

He didn't know anything could feel as bad as being shot and left for dead. What he was experiencing now, though, was a thousand times worse. This was his chance of happiness slipping through his fingers.

CHAPTER
Eleven

THE REST of the week didn't get much better for Max. He arrived at work every morning to work out, usually with the SWAT team.

Depending on what asshole mouthed off about Karlie depended on what shit job he got after straightening the man out. Usually it involved him walking most of the day through the worst parts of town. If he got to actually pop someone in the face for a comment, he pulled an extra shift at night. So far, he had worked most nights.

He hadn't had a chance to tell his mother or sister what had happened, but somehow they knew. Every night when he crawled home too tired to care about eating, he found something waiting for him in the fridge. For the first time in his life, they had chosen to stay quiet about the entire thing.

Max wished he really could work himself to death. It would be much easier than feeling his heart shatter a little more each day.

There wasn't a moment of the day when he didn't think about her and every night, she smiled up at him in his dreams. By the end of the week, the comments aimed at him had slowly dwindled. He guessed they had gotten bored with dodging his fist every day.

Oddly, the SWAT guys were the only ones that didn't seem interested in giving him crap about it. They continued to make room for him when he reported to work out as ordered.

By the weekend, Max was ready for a day off. His mother had called to invite him to dinner, refusing to accept the word no for an answer. Walking the block to her house, he was greeted by a squeal when he walked in the door.

"Maxim!" Chiara yelled before throwing her arms around his neck. "I figured out how to get my iPad to connect to the television so we can watch Karlie's game tonight." Max felt his heart shatter again. How many times could it do that before he finally gave up. Turning him loose, she bounced back into the living room.

"How are you, Max?" his mother asked, her knowing eyes sizing him up.

"I'm fine," he answered, automatically moving to the cabinets to pull out plates.

"You don't look fine." He ignored her as he started setting the table. It wouldn't help anything to discuss it. He had done what was best for Karlie. How he felt didn't matter.

"I made your favorite," she said at his back, changing the subject.

"It smells good." Helping her set the food on the table, he waited until Chiara had joined them before getting a small serving. He also didn't want to tell her that he hadn't been eating that much lately. "How's school?" At the very least, he could pretend he wanted to be here.

"It's good. I think I have mostly As, except for Chemistry." Max tried to listen as his sister rambled on about classes, her friends, and the latest gossip. He had almost managed to tune her out when she said something that brought his head up sharply.

"I talked to Karlie yesterday before they left."

"How did she look?" he asked.

"Sad, Max. She just looks sad. She said she wished you could be there. She said she would remember not to kiss you this time."

Max stood, pushing his chair back hard enough it crashed to the ground. Picking it back up, he set it carefully at the table before turning toward the door.

"I need some air," he said, pushing outside. He made it around his motorcycle to the fence before sinking to the ground. *He* had made her sad, it was his fault. Closing his eyes, he almost didn't feel the body that slid down next to him.

"Max," his sister said quietly. "I don't know what I'm supposed to do to help fix this."

"Chi, there's nothing you can do. I almost got her suspended from school right before finals. I'm the reason she now has a letter in her file that the law schools will see when she tries to get in. I'm the one who fucked this up."

She slid her arms around him, resting her head on his shoulder. "Isn't there a way to unfuck this?"

"I don't think so. I certainly don't know how." She sighed, hugging him tighter as his heart shattered for the hundredth time. It might not be so bad if he couldn't feel the pain rip through him every time he thought about Karlie.

"Come on, let's go watch the game." Helping her up, Max followed his sister back into the house. His mother had put the food away but was currently placing an assortment of cannoli on a plate. Kissing her cheek, Max poured them each some coffee before settling on the couch.

Watching the game wasn't as bad as he was afraid it would be. They had won their first game earlier in the day before losing the one he was watching. Even in defeat, he was amazed by Karlie's poise as she accepted the hand slaps of the other team. She had played just as hard as she always had, which made his chest swell with pride.

Watching Chiara type out a message to Karlie telling her how proud they were of her, he ached to do the same. But he hadn't lied to his sister. He had no idea how to unfuck this up, so he simply watched their conversation fly.

Finally making it out of the house with three Tupperware containers of food and a promise to make it to mass tomorrow, Max breathed a sigh of relief when he shut his door. He had no intention of holding up his promise, instead he planned to hit the heavy bag at the police gym until his mind went numb. It was the only way he could think to make it through the day until work started again on Monday.

When Monday rolled around, his shoulders were sore from the heavy bag as he maxed out on squats. By Tuesday, he barely noticed his shoulders anymore when he benched more than he ever had. On Wednesday, he broke his own record, running fifteen miles on the treadmill. Thursday, he broke that record by five miles.

It seemed, though, the harder he worked, the more he thought about her. Wasn't extreme exercise supposed to have the opposite effect? By the end of the following week, he was positive he was losing his mind.

"Scaletti. Mason wants you in his office." Max had been in the middle of pushing weights on a sled across the room with the guys from SWAT when one of the clerks summoned him. Shit, now what had he done? They probably needed a male prostitute for a sting operation and he was the obvious choice.

Receiving a head nod from the team leader, he sighed, heading toward the office wing. Reaching his commander's office, he was waved through by the secretary.

"You wanted to see me, sir?" Max asked, pushing open the door.

"Come in." Max walked in front of the desk, standing at

attention. He noticed another man sitting to his left. A moment later, the door opened when the team leader he had just been working out with walked inside. Closing the door behind him, he took his place next to it, crossing his arms over his chest.

"Max, this is Commander Taylor of SWAT."

"Commander," he said with a nod. Settling back in his chair, the man opened a file he had lying on his lap.

"I see you've been with the department around five years now. Got a dispensation to join a year before the minimum age. Worked patrol for a year before being transferred to the gang task force division. You've received several commendations as well as a distinguished service award while there."

Max glanced over at him, wondering why his career was being reviewed. Wouldn't they have already fired him if they were going to?

"According to the reports, you were removed from the task force having been shot after a CI informed on you. You were then assigned temporarily after completing the necessary training, to one of the local college campuses for a year. You managed to stay there for a little over three months before being sent back pending disciplinary action for having an inappropriate relationship with one of the students."

"Sir," Max began, but quieted when the commander held a finger up at him, still looking at the file.

"As you can imagine, neither your lieutenant nor I were happy to have this show up on his desk."

Max closed his eyes briefly. God, he felt sick. Even as a kid, all he had ever wanted to be was a cop. However, why they needed two guys from the SWAT unit to fire him was beyond his imagination. Did they think he would lose his shit? After the thumpings he had delved out in the locker room, maybe they did.

"So tell me something," Commander Taylor continued, "what did you do to get more than just a warning?"

Max stood silently, trying to think. He couldn't remember ever getting a warning from walking her home or eating lunch together. More than likely, there was someone at that game that demanded more, the dean of students most likely. He was sure he had made the police captain on campus look bad, but he didn't remember seeing him at the game.

"Come on, man. Did you fuck her against the stacks in the library?"

"No, sir!"

"Cop a feel during an assembly?" Max could feel himself starting to get pissed. They could talk about him all they wanted, but don't talk about Karlie like she's a slut.

"No, sir!"

"He's assured me there was nothing that could blow back on us in the future," Lieutenant Mason answered. "Matter of fact, I met the young woman briefly. Didn't seem like the type to be coerced into anything."

Commander Taylor closed the file, studying Max intently until he could swear he felt the sweat rolling down his back. Finally, the commander shifted in his chair to look at the team leader by the door. Max couldn't see what they communicated between them, but the commander turned back to him quickly.

"We have an opening in SWAT. The team thinks you would make an excellent candidate to fill that spot if you're interested in trying out." Wait, what?

"Normally we have an open tryout for positions, but this time we would like to see what you're made of first. You'll have to pass the preliminary physical and mental evals, but until those can be arranged, you will report to Troy standing behind you. Are you interested?"

"Yes, sir." How did he go from being punished by getting the shit patrols to bypassing the rigorous, extremely competitive tryouts of SWAT?

"When you're done here, report to the locker rooms. Troy

will get your training gear and go over your schedule."
Standing, Commander Taylor reached out his hand to shake
Max's. "Welcome to SWAT." Walking to the door, Taylor
turned before he followed Troy out.

"Oh and, officer," Max turned to look at him, "cut the
fighting bullshit out in the locker room." Without waiting for
an answer, he walked out, closing the door behind him.

"Sit down," Mason said, pointing to the chair that had just
been vacated. Max slowly sank down into the chair. He still
couldn't wrap his head around what had just happened.
SWAT was such an elite squad in this department, he never
even considered making it on the team. He knew guys that
tried out every year that were better cops than him.

"Listen up, I sang your damn praises when he inquired
about you. Don't fuck this up."

"Yes, sir. Thank you. I won't."

"Go get your black wardrobe," Mason dismissed him
without a second look until he reached the door. "Max?"

"Sir?" he said turning.

"Good luck."

"Thank you, sir," he said, leaving.

By the time he made it back to the SWAT offices, Troy was
waiting with his training uniforms and schedule. Instead of
the usual training camp that most officers trying out for
SWAT go through, they were going to train him themselves.

He was informed what boots he would need to purchase
when he left and how much he needed to budget for the
actual unit uniforms. Looking at the schedule, he saw he
would begin training on the high-powered weapons they
used tomorrow after workout.

"Any questions?" Troy asked when he was finished with
the brief orientation.

"Not so far."

"Good. You know all the team since you've been working
out with them for two weeks now. You've got a week before

testing begins so we'll see you back here first thing Monday morning. Have a good weekend. Welcome to SWAT." Max gave him a chin lift before Troy walked out.

He really wanted to whoop with a fist bump to the air, but he fought the urge, wanting to play it cool even more. Shit, he wanted to call everyone he knew to tell them he was asked to try out. Most of all, he wanted to tell Karlie. He could almost guarantee he would receive another jump into his arms with a kiss.

With a sigh, he closed his new locker, running his hand over the new piece of tape with his name on it.

————

Karlie was just sad. It was the best way to describe how empty she felt. Sam had worked hard to bolster her happiness, but honestly, Karlie didn't want to be bolstered.

She had secretly hoped all week before the start of the NCAA tournament that she would hear from Max, but she hadn't. Then she hoped, with all of the spotlight off of the team, he would call her, but he didn't. It was now three weeks since he had told her they shouldn't see each other and her heart had begun to crumble.

Chiara told her that he had watched her games, but didn't give her anything else about how he was doing. Karlie wasn't stupid. She was positive Max had finally just grown tired of putting up with the college drama that seemed to always surround her. He was a man out in the real world, it would certainly be much easier for him to find someone his own age.

Everybody's advice was just to forget him. She had tried her best, but it just wasn't that easy. Everything on this stupid campus reminded her of Max. The picnic table they used to eat at, the police office, a motorcycle driving by, even the empty fire extinguisher still sitting in their back stairwell.

How did you get over someone when they had become the most important thing in your life?

She simply continued to fake it as she numbly went to class or hung out with friends. Sam had even confided to her one late night that this was why she would never get close enough to a man to hurt this bad.

It had been one of Karlie's bad nights. Gemma had been so nasty that night that Karlie had slept on the floor of Sam's room. Now her only hope of surviving until Christmas was by hiding in the library when not in class.

"So we have mice," Sam said, flopping down on the couch in the corner of the library's first floor where Karlie was currently working on a paper. "They're really more like Chihuahuas running through the kitchen."

"Gross," Karlie said, looking over her reading glasses. "Did you call housing?"

"Yep. They're bringing us traps in... guess."

"Three to four days." Sam pointed her finger guns at Karlie with a wink. "Great, what are we supposed to do until then?"

"Train them to perform circus acts? How would I know?"

"It was more of a rhetorical question."

Sam sat up, studying Karlie. Was she waiting to see if her friend would finally fall apart?

With a fortifying breath, Karlie sat up, squaring her shoulders as she shoved her stuff back into her backpack. What was she doing? She didn't roll over and play dead just because some man dumped her when things got to be too much. She had just helped win a fucking championship, damn it.

"Fuck it, let's go get something to eat."

With a grin, her best friend stood up. "I know just the place."

Walking into Donnelly's fifteen minutes later, Karlie

avoided their 'regular' table, opting for one of the smaller booths along the back wall.

"Hey, ladies. What brings you down on a quiet week-night?" Parker asked, walking up to their table.

"We are in need of the biggest, sloppiest burgers you can get us. Complete with pub chips, onion rings, and Cokes," Sam ordered, dazzling him with her best smile.

"Anyone else joining you. Where's the cop?" Parker asked, writing their order down.

"They had a parting of the ways."

"Huh, that's too bad. He was okay for a cop. No one else showing up then?"

"Nope. Looking for someone in particular?" Sam waited as Parker looked up at them.

"No, just making sure. I'll put your order in." Returning his pencil to its regular spot behind his ear, he turned to Karlie. "Sorry, sweetheart. He looked really into you."

Turning, they watched as he walked back to the bar. "I don't know. Astrid might be right about that ass." Karlie laughed at Sam, remembering their shy friend throwing a quarter at him.

"Speaking of, I think he might have a crush on her. After y'all went back to the apartment on Halloween, he asked about her."

"Really?" Sam answered in a conspiratorial tone. "I guess I won't let my wounded pride at him striking me down sting so bad anymore."

"You hit on the bartender?"

"Have you seen him, Karlie? Of course I hit on the bartender. He was very nice when he brushed me off. You know the front view isn't too shabby either."

"Sam!"

"Karlie! Tell me that wasn't one of the first things you checked out on Max."

They both stopped talking when Parker set their drinks on

the table, grinning at him. It morphed into a strange look of concern as he backed away. They gave a small wave as he turned around.

"Anyway, ten bucks says he never acts on it," Sam continued. Karlie sat for a moment studying Sam before looking over at the bar where Parker pulled a draft from the tap for one of his customers.

"I'll take that bet." Shaking hands, they laughed when Parker reappeared with their food.

"Are you sure you haven't already been drinking?" he asked, sliding their plates in front of them. "You look like you're planning a bank heist over here."

"No, nothing that sinister. But if we do, can we count you in?" Sam teased.

"Definitely. Just as long as I don't have to wear pantyhose over my face." He grinned when they both laughed. "Okay, I'll check on you in a bit. You know where I am if you need anything. Just wave."

"Thanks, Parker," they chimed out in unison.

Digging into her burger, Karlie felt like she hadn't eaten in years. Neither one of them said a word until they had plowed through most of the food. Karlie was just starting to debate if she could pull off unbuttoning the top button on her jeans when a giant piece of bread pudding covered in a whiskey sauce was placed on the table. Looking up, she stared at two boys who looked just alike.

"Hi, my brother said it was cool if I brought you some dessert," the one said with a smile. "On the house, of course," he was quick to add.

"Yeah, for winning the conference championship. We streamed it," the other one said, stepping out from behind what had to be his twin.

"He also said not to say anything about breaking up with your boyfriend, but I think that might be why he let us add a second piece to the plate," the first one whispered. "Don't tell him we said anything."

"Promise," Karlie said, sitting up with a smile. "I'm Karlie. This is Sam. This looks delicious, thank whoever your brother is for us, please. And don't worry, your secret is safe with us."

"I'm Liam. This is Ronan. Our brother is Parker," the one said, answering by waving his hand at the bar. "Okay, he said not to hover, so congratulations, we're sorry, and enjoy." With an enthusiastic nod from his twin, Liam spun, retreating toward the back.

"Okay, they were fucking adorable. Wonder how old they are."

"Sam." Karlie shook her head at her friend as she took a bite. "But who would have thought he would have such young brothers. He has to be like thirty, right?"

"I would think so, though beards and tattoos always make guys look older so who knows." Sam popped a spoonful into her mouth. "God, this stuff is good," she mumbled around chewing. "Maybe that's what you need to get what's-his-name out of your mind. A bad boy."

"His name is Max and I don't think that's the answer."

"I really wish there was something I could do. It's killing me seeing you this unhappy."

"Don't worry, I'll get better. Just need some time." Reaching across the table, Sam squeezed her hand before they both settled back in to conquering the mound of dessert in front of them.

CHAPTER
Twelve

MAX WAS EXHAUSTED. He spent the week training harder than he even thought possible. Each day started with an enhanced workout followed by tactical training. When his shift was over, he tried to work in more time on the range before heading home to study for the upcoming test.

He worked tirelessly on learning the equipment required to safely breach any situation. Being the man on the team to determine how to enter any structure while still maintaining the safety of his team was daunting.

Today, they spent the afternoon at their urban training facility, running through live scenarios. He managed to outwit a hostage situation, dropping them through a ceiling, storm a classroom without casualties, and even raid a crack house full of weapons.

However, he had failed spectacularly at finding the hidden threat in an alley leading to the 'death' of his entire team. His punishment had been a good ass ripping from Troy.

He followed the rest of the team into the locker room to change before leaving for the day. Reaching his locker, he pulled out his phone to check for messages. Okay, really just one message.

He shook his head, tossing his phone back in his locker. Why did he expect her to contact him when he had ended it weeks ago? Still, he always held out hope.

"Max, are you going to have your head on straight for Monday?" Troy asked, standing at a locker on the far side. Monday was the day they decided if he was either going to continue with SWAT or forever remain a patrolman.

"What's up with his head?" one of the other guys asked.

"Major case of blue balls if you ask me," another one answered. There were five other guys on his team with a total of approximately fifteen men total including the K-9 unit.

"Have you not made up with that girl yet?" Troy asked, pulling a dry T-shirt over his head.

"It's not that simple. I completely fucked everything up. She's still on probation and I don't want to do anything to get her kicked out." Max sat down on the bench that lined the wall opposite of the lockers.

"I didn't think you were still working over there."

"I'm not, but they put a letter in her file that will hurt her chances of getting into law school if she decides to go that route. I thought, maybe if she keeps her nose clean until she graduates they might remove it."

"That's already been taken care of." When Max looked at Troy in confusion, he continued. "Yeah, Taylor went to school with the dean. He had that removed last week."

"So, what I hear is this. You got some hot, young coed on the hook with no reason to stay away from her. Am I right?" one of the guys asked.

"Davis is right. You don't work over there now so you're no longer on the staff. As long as she's over eighteen, they can't tell her who to date. Seems pretty easy to unfuck."

Max sat in silence, trying to work out what they were saying. Could it really be that simple?

"I'm sure she's moved on by now," he said dismissively, standing back up to pack his bag.

"But what if she hasn't?" Davis answered. "Something to think about." He was right. What if she hadn't? What if, even if she had, he got her back anyway?

"That got his wheels spinning. Come on guys, let's head out for a beer. Looks like the newbie has somewhere else to be." With a chin lift at Max, Troy led the rest of the team out of the locker room.

Max sat for a minute, thinking. Did he dare go get her back? Fuck yeah, he did.

Quickly grabbing his stuff before he could change his mind, he checked his watch to figure out where she would be. With any luck, if he hurried, he could catch her coming out of her last class for the day. Slamming the locker closed, Max jogged out of the building toward the parking lot, carrying his helmet in his hand.

He raced out of the parking lot, heading across town like the devil himself was after him. Approaching campus, he pulled onto the sidewalk off of the main street so he didn't block traffic while he searched for her among the other students.

Easing his bike toward the center of campus, he didn't care if he got in trouble for driving on the sidewalks. He needed to find her. Scanning the students walking through the mall from classes or toward dinner, he finally saw a flash of long hair the color of cinnamon pulled up in a ponytail. As if in slow motion, she turned around, her amber eyes lighting up at him.

Stopping the motorcycle, he climbed off, unbuckling his helmet. There could have been other students around. There must have been since he handed his helmet to someone as he walked toward her. It didn't matter, he couldn't see anyone else. Her perfect mouth opened slightly on a gasp as he stormed across the mall.

They could kick him out of SWAT, take away his apartment, lock him up forever if they wanted. None of it was worth it anyway without her there next to him.

He vaguely noticed her friends take a step back as he approached, but he didn't slow down. Reaching a hand into her hair, he pulled her lips against his in one motion. The instant she melted against him, he felt his shattered heart pick itself up off the ground.

He poured everything he had into kissing her. Reaching down with his hands, he pulled her off the ground. She wrapped her legs around his waist, right where they had always belonged. When he finally felt his vision start to narrow from lack of oxygen, he pulled back to look into her eyes. She grinned at him as a roar of applause and catcalls erupted around them.

"What are you doing?" she asked breathlessly.

"I'm unfucking this up," he replied. Karlie looked at him like she was searching for something. Max felt his heart pounding in his chest, waiting for her to say something, anything.

"Did you know the first record of the word fuck is found in the margins of a manuscript by Cicero?" she asked.

Max grinned. "Fuck, I fucking missed you."

Pulling her back in, he kissed her again as she clung to him as if her life depended on it. Finally, he let her slide down until she was standing on the ground again.

"What changed, Max?" she asked, looking up at him.

"Yeah, Max. We'd all kind of like to know that?" Sam glared at him. Max knew she would be the hardest to convince he wasn't going to flake again. Looking around, he noticed that most of her friends were standing around them. He wondered for a second how his sister had gotten his helmet.

"If I promise to explain everything over dinner tomorrow night, can we wait until then?" Max asked, looking at the other girls starting to form a protective wall around Karlie. Even his sister was scowling at him. Sam looked at the rest of the group for a minute before answering.

"Fine, but we pick the place. This had better be a damn good story." Holding up his hands in surrender, he turned back to Karlie.

"Do you have anything else you need to do tonight? Can we go somewhere to talk?" he asked, wishing the rest of the group would drift off.

"Yeah, we can do that." Turning to Sam, she handed off her backpack. "I'll text later, okay?"

With one more stink face aimed at Max, Sam hugged Karlie before walking toward the apartment. As if they were operating as one unit, the rest of Karlie's friends followed her. Max felt his shoulders physically sag in relief.

"So what are you feeding me?"

"Mexican?"

"Good start." Taking his hand, she headed to his motorcycle.

———

Karlie hadn't known what to expect from today, but it certainly wasn't Max riding up like some black knight to sweep her off her feet. She had met up with everyone on the mall after class to discuss what they wanted to do for dinner when she heard the faint rumble of a motorcycle approaching.

Turning, she had been shocked to see him getting off the seat. But when he whipped off his helmet, handing it to some random student as he bared down on her, she had completely lost her ability to think. She only had a moment to take him in as he stomped at her like she was a mission he had to accomplish.

In the weeks they had been apart, he had changed. He was even more ripped than he had been before. His black T-shirt strained to contain the extra layer of muscle he had put on. There wasn't a female, or male for that matter, that didn't miss the chance to take in the wall of man walking toward her.

Expecting an awkward attempt at conversation, she was peeled from the little remaining brain cells still firing when he swept her in for a kiss that blazed through her body like an inferno. Those lightning storms that swept through her home-town in Texas had nothing on the sparks that raced through her body at that kiss.

If this was Max's way of saying their time being apart was over, he had made quite the impact. Was this feeling the reason he hadn't stopped her from kissing him at the confer-ence tournament?

Climbing on the motorcycle behind him, Karlie reveled in the way his body felt as she slid her hands under his T-shirt to rest on his bare stomach. She grinned at the startled motion he made, the same way he always did. Even though he appeared to be Max 2.0 now, she loved that she could still keep him off balance.

Pulling into her favorite Mexican food restaurant, Max helped her remove her helmet. Leading her inside, he waited until they were settled into a booth against the back wall before speaking.

"I was told Commander Taylor had the letter of repri-mand removed from your file."

"Who's Commander Taylor?"

"He's the head of the SWAT unit. He went to school with the dean or something. Anyway, you don't have to worry about that anymore."

"Okay, that's good." Karlie looked down at her menu. It seemed now the awkward part began.

Making her decision on what to eat, she closed her menu,

looking up to find Max studying her from across the table. She felt her face heat, although she had no idea why.

Clearing his throat, he looked out into the restaurant before continuing.

"So after all the shit hit the fan, I think my lieutenant set out to kill me. He doubled my workout by sending me over to the SWAT workout after completing my regulation one. After I was done there, he sent me on the worst patrols you can be assigned in this city. I wrestled several knife-toting crackheads to the ground, got rocks thrown at me and was even propositioned a couple times while in uniform."

He stopped his story when the waitress arrived to get their order. When she left, Karlie started to tell him she was glad she hadn't known those details or it would have killed her with worry when he began speaking again.

"Anyway, for some reason, I was called into his office a couple weeks later to be grilled by the SWAT commander over what happened to get me fired from campus duty. They decided I might be a good candidate to be on a team and wanted to make sure our situation wouldn't blow back on them."

"I'm so sorry, Max," Karlie whispered.

Max brought his eyes back to her from where they had been staring out into the restaurant.

"You don't have anything to be sorry for. Like I told them, we didn't do anything wrong. I guess they were good with that because they invited me to start training with them. It's really hard work, but I love it.

"Problem is, I guess my mind isn't where it needs to be because I keep fucking up. It was pointed out at the end of shift today that there was a simple solution to my problem. I just needed to go get my girl back."

"Max," Karlie began, not having any idea where the sentence was going. Max, I don't want to be hurt anymore? Max, I want to marry you and have as many babies as you're willing to put in me? Max, did you know cheese is the most stolen food in the world?

Relief flooded her, when he interrupted, saving her from what promised to be the worst sentence ever.

"I'm sorry. I just wanted to see if there was a chance we could start over," he said.

Before she could answer, the waitress arrived with her dinner. It gave her the chance she needed to think about her answer. Did she want to still be with Max? Oh hell yes, without a doubt. But how did she see that proceeding forward?

When the waitress had refilled their drinks, tried her best to flirt with Max and then finally drifted off when he was obviously uninterested, she forked a big bite of her cheese enchilada.

"Max," she said when she had finished her bite, noticing that he was just moving his food around on his plate. That was almost criminal, it was Mexican food, after all, it demanded to be eaten. "What if I don't want to start over?"

"Oh," he said in resignation.

"No, I mean, what if I want to pick right back up from where we were? I don't want to go back to that first date stuff. Besides, I've exhausted my knowledge of nipple rings. I want to move right on into hot rolls in the sack." She stared at him in fascination as he seemed to take every inch of his lung capacity, moaning the word fuck out.

"Can we just do that? You know," she said, lowering her voice looking around. "Whatever comes after what you did the last time I was at your apartment before all this crap started." She worried when he continued to stare at her in fixed shock. Finally shaking his head, he pointed his fork at her dinner.

"Eat faster. Ma'am!" he called out, waving at their server. "We'll take that check now."

Karlie laughed as he plowed into his meal like a man on a

mission. That seemed to be a thing with him today, missions. She had to admit, she liked the new bigger, badder Max.

She felt a shiver of anticipation run down her spine. Had she just asked him for sex? Well, whatever she had done, he was just going to have to cool his heels. After all, her plate was filled with enchiladas. They were meant to be savored.

CHAPTER
Thirteen

MAX THOUGHT he would explode watching Karlie leisurely finish her plate of what looked like a whole lot of mess covered in cheese to him. He wasn't sure he would ever get used to her extreme love of Mexican food, but he was willing to try.

Did she really just say she would rather speed things up than start over? He wasn't complaining. He would much rather watch her riding his cock half the night than drop her politely at her door.

"What are you thinking so hard about?" she asked, startling him out of his head. He couldn't exactly admit he was calculating the number of condoms he had in his apartment.

"I was trying to remember if I had any ice cream in the freezer at home." Sure, that sounded plausible.

"Do we need to stop and pick some up?"

"Nope," he answered quickly. "Done?" Laughing, Karlie placed her napkin next to her plate. Standing, Max reached out, taking her hand to pull her out of the booth. He had already paid the bill. "Are you warm enough or do you want my jacket?"

"I'm good, I'll just snuggle up behind you until we get

there." With a smile that lit up her eyes, she looked up at him. Reaching down, he zipped up her coat before smoothing a lock of her hair behind her ear.

When he had her helmet snug, he straddled the bike balancing it as she swung up behind him. How did he think he could have survived without her touching him? It still felt like the first time she wrapped her arms around him, trusting he would keep her safe.

"This looks fantastic, Max," Karlie said as he hung their coats on a hook by the door when they finally made it back to his apartment.

"You think?" He turned to look around. No, it had looked just okay before. Now it looked perfect, with her standing in the middle of it. "I finally got everything done with some help. Chiara and Mom keep sneaking over here with crap to decorate with."

"Well, they've done a great job." Karlie laughed, looking through the door into the bedroom. "They managed to make it masculine without it looking like a man cave."

"Yeah, no light saber nightlights or dogs playing poker," he said with a smile, stalking toward her. Was it too soon to throw her against the wall and fuck her senseless?

Catching up to her as she looked around the kitchen, he pulled her against him as he slowly bent down to brush her lips with his.

"Well, there's always room for a light saber," she breathed out on a shaky breath when he pulled back. "Did you know the noise they make comes from combining the hum of a tube-type television and a film projector?"

Reaching down to wrap his hands around her waist, Max set her on the counter before stepping between her legs.

"How much time do you spend on Google?" he asked as he nipped at her bottom lip, drawing a gasp from her.

Taking full advantage, he slipped his tongue inside her mouth, exploring every part as her tongue tentatively tangled with his. Sliding a hand into her hair, he pulled her head to the side so he could nip his way down her neck to her shoulder.

Returning to her mouth, he slid his hand under her shirt, growling when he found her hard nipple. He had one thought running through his brain borrowed directly from his seventeen-year-old self. Get in her pants and don't blow before you get there.

Somewhere, though, in the one percent of his brain still trying to function on logical thought, he noticed something wasn't quite right. Sliding his hand back down to her waist, he pulled back, studying her with a concerned crease between his eyebrows.

She looked like a fucking wet dream with her puffy lips and mussed hair where he had slid it out of its hairband. But she was also shaking slightly with her eyes closed. When he didn't continue, she slowly opened her eyes.

"Did you want to stop?" he asked, holding his breath. What he really wanted to ask was 'do you mind if I turn you over so I can fuck you against this counter.'

"I don't know." Whoa, that put the brakes on in a hurry in his mind. Taking a step back, he leaned against the sink, grabbing the sides with both hands hard enough his knuckles turned white.

"No," she added. He cocked his head at her in question. "Maybe?"

With a sigh, she sat for a second in thought before unloading. "I don't know what I'm doing. What if I do it wrong? I mean, should I keep my eyes open or close them, where do my hands go, do I need to take your clothes off, do you want a blow job first? Don't look at me like that."

"Look like what?" he asked, trying to convince his eyebrows to return from where they had disappeared somewhere near his hairline in surprise.

"Like you think I'm insane."

"That's because you are insane!" When her shoulders straightened as she glared at him, he shook his head with a chuckle. "You know, while you're thinking all of that, I have one thought going through my brain like a mantra. Don't blow, don't blow, like I'm some fucking teenager. You do remember you've already gotten off rubbing all over me, right?"

"Max, don't get mad at me." Max jerked back in surprise. Taking a step forward, he gripped her chin, bringing it up until her eyes would meet his.

"I'm not mad, baby. I'm just astounded at how your mind works. It's part of what I love about you." Turning loose of her chin, he stepped back to the sink again. Studying her, he had an idea. "Do you trust me?"

"Of course I trust you. You've saved my life twice now."

"I think I have an idea. You have all these questions racing through that sexy brain of yours. I'm going to take at least one of those decisions away from you. Stay here." Brushing his lips over hers, Max turned to walk into the bedroom.

Returning with one of his ties, he looped it around her head, securing it on the side so she didn't have to lie on a knot.

"Now," he whispered, running the back of his knuckles over her face as she trembled. "All you have to think about is telling me what you want me to do differently or what you want more of. Okay?"

"Okay. But, Max?"

"Yeah, sweetheart?" He pulled her hands behind her, placing them in one of his hands as he placed gentle kisses down her neck. "You...you won't plow into me too hard, right?"

Max stood up to look at her. Good Jesus, where in the hell did this woman get her information? Didn't matter, he could turn that question to his advantage.

"Plow into you, baby? Yeah, someday I'll plow into you. It

will probably be after a hard day at work. Maybe we had to drop into a building where children were being held hostage."

He heard a gasp when he leaned down, running his tongue down the shell of her ear, sucking the lobe into his mouth. Releasing it, he ran his hands under her shirt, releasing her hands so he could ease it over her head.

"We'll save them all, of course, but I'll be so full of adrenaline it'll take everything I have to make it home. You'll be coming out of the shower after a hard practice wrapped in a towel."

Bending, he licked her nipple through her bra before sucking it into his mouth through the material.

"Max," she moaned, arching her back. "Then what happens?" He smiled, releasing her nipple. Looking up, he found her mouth slightly open as her breaths started to come out in little pants.

"You'll walk over to give me a kiss hello before turning around to get dressed. But I've been dreaming about your wet pussy wrapped around my cock all day, so I grab you by the wrist before you can get too far. I look at the table, debating if I want to bend you face down onto it so I can fuck you from behind, but it's too far away."

She moaned when he rolled her taught bud between his fingers. Catching her moan with his mouth as his tongue insisted it needed to explore more, he ran his hand up her back slowly until he reached the clasp of her bra, releasing it.

"Do we go to the table anyway?" she whispered when he was done with her mouth.

Pulling her to him, he picked her up from the counter. With a squeal of surprise, she wrapped her legs around his waist, her arms around his neck, as he carried her into the bedroom. Laying her down gently, he followed her down, careful to not crush her.

"It's too far. My cock is begging to be buried deep inside

you, and I can't deny it any longer. My hand moves to your throat as I pull your back against my chest. Holding you in my grasp, I rip the towel from your body."

Tracing a path down her neck with his tongue, he worked his way down to her nipple, straining for his touch. She would just have to wait for more of the story, they demanded his attention. Pinning her hands above her head, he drove her crazy, nipping and sucking until she started to squirm under him.

"Please," she begged.

With a smile, he released her nipple, kissing down to her stomach, dipping his tongue into her navel as it quivered. Kneeling between her legs, he continued his story as he pulled his shirt over his head. He still needed to work her boots off and figure out how to peel the leggings from her body.

"You struggle for a moment when I suck your soft skin where your shoulder meets your neck into my mouth. But only until my fingers find your clit, making a circle before they plunge into you. I have to always remember to make sure you're ready for me, but I shouldn't have worried. You're always wet for me."

He had managed to get the boots off before backing off the end of the bed, sliding the leggings off as he went. When they were lying on the floor, followed by her panties, he wrapped his hands around her legs, pulling her to the edge.

"Yes, Max. Like that, like that," Karlie moaned when he ran his tongue through her folds, pressing down as he circled her clit. She tried to arch her back, wanting more, but he laid a large hand on her belly, holding her still. He needed her drenched, but he would get her there on his own terms.

Sliding one of her legs over his shoulder, he circled his tongue around her entrance before thrusting it in with a growl. Reaching his hand up, he pressed his thumb against her clit, rubbing it until she moaned his name, coming on his tongue.

"Move back up the bed," he instructed when she had recovered.

Standing, he added the rest of his clothes to the growing pile on the floor.

"Are we done? Will you at least finish your story?" Even though Karlie's eyes were still hidden by his tie, he shook his head at her anyway.

"We're not even close to done," he whispered into her ear as he bent over her. "But I'll tell you more of the story." It would be impossible to remember where the story had left off if he hadn't spent hours playing through it in his mind at night.

"You're dripping all over my hand as you beg me to fill you. Pushing you against the wall next to the door, I can't wait any longer. As you wrap your leg around me, I bend, shoving my hard cock inside until my balls slap against your body. My name rips from your lips and you struggle to find the leverage you need to ride me, but you're not in charge. I am."

Levering between her thighs, he licked along the seam of her lips until she granted him access to her mouth again. As he explored her mouth, never seeming to get enough, he rocked his hips, running his shaft through her folds, swallowing her moans.

When he was sure he couldn't continue for even another second without coming, he sat back on his knees between her thighs. Grinning when her eyebrows knit in frustration above her blindfold, he reached down, untying it.

"I need you to tell me you want this," he said, staring into her blinking eyes. She nodded, closing them as she reached for him. Catching her wrist in his hands, he pinned them next to her.

"Karlie, open your eyes and tell me you want me inside

you." He needed to be sure she was still on board. They didn't get a do-over if she changed her mind later. Piercing him with the most incredible lust-filled amber eyes, she smiled at him.

"I need you inside me, Max. I love you, I need you to make me yours." Max felt his once shattered heart swell to twice its size. Fuck yeah, she was his. Every fantastic inch of her.

Without another word, he leaned over to the nightstand, grabbing one of the condoms he had tossed there when he had grabbed the tie from his closet. When it was on, he shoved her legs wider, running himself through her folds again as he kissed her.

"Relax and breathe," he whispered in her ear. Reaching between them, he lined himself up with her entrance, easing the head inside. Karlie took a big gulp of air, scrambling to wrap her legs around his hips. Pushing farther in, he stopped when she started holding her breath, only taking in small pants.

"Babe, you need to relax. You have my cock so strangled, it's debating asking for reinforcements." When she barked out a laugh, he thrust the rest of the way in.

"Oh, god," she gasped. "Is it always this big?"

"Well, mine is," he answered, desperately trying to stay still until she could adjust. He fully expected to hear some statistic about cock size, but Karlie simply slowed her breathing until she settled against him.

"Are you okay?"

"Yes," she answered. Slowly he pulled partway out before easing back in. "Oh my god," she moaned, pulling a small smile from his lips. The next time he did it she responded with, "Yes, sir."

He had to admit, he had never had sex like this. It was so far better than anything he had ever done, it even surpassed those fantasies that had sustained him over the last several months.

Soon, he was pulling almost all the way out before slamming back into her. He could feel his balls starting to tighten as he reached between them, balancing on one arm. Finding her clit, he pinched it, feeling her muscles clamp down as she rolled her hips up to meet his thrust. He knew she wasn't quite there yet, but if she didn't hurry, it would be too late for him.

Rubbing her clit faster as he pounded into her, he pinched it one more time. Feeling her clench around him like a fist milking him for everything she had as she screamed his name, he managed to thrust twice more before feeling his climax roll through his body.

Pulling his hand from between them, he just managed to catch himself before crashing down on top of her. His body forced him to thrust into her several more times before it was empty.

Opening his eyes when his senses returned, he found her smiling up at him. Her eyes were heavy with exhaustion, her skin flushed from her orgasm and her mane of hair spread in a wild halo around her. Max knew he was done waiting for someone to come into his life. She was right here.

"You're so fucking amazing," he said, bending down to place a soft kiss on her lips. "I'm not letting you go."

"It's going to be hard for you to work like this," Karlie answered with a grin. Max laughed, stopping abruptly when she winced. "Things jerk when you laugh."

"Sorry, relax and I'll get off of you."

"How do I relax?" That one had him stumped. It didn't help that his cock wanted to go another round. With a deep breath, he worked back out of her as she shut her eyes tightly. "Ouch."

"I'm sorry. Wait there, I'll get something to clean you up with." Max saw her turn a bright shade of red as he turned toward the bathroom. After taking care of the condom, he ran warm water on a washcloth, returning to the bedroom. Coaxing her legs apart while the red on her body increased, he gently wiped her clean.

Max didn't like how embarrassed she was, since all he wanted to do was get on his knees and worship her. She pulled the covers up to cover herself the second he was done. No, he wasn't okay with this. It was his mess, she needed to get used to him taking care of her every time.

Standing next to the bed, he studied her for a moment. If he was going to marry her someday, he had better start now trying to work his way through the maze that was Karlie's mind.

"Hey, I have another idea."

"Okay," she answered, a little leery. Fair enough, last time he said that she wound up here.

"I'm pretty sure there's ice cream in the freezer. With all of the strenuous activity, I think the Mexican food might be making a repeat visit." Karlie laughed and relaxed a little. "Let me toss you something to put on if you'll go get us some. We can climb under the covers and watch a movie."

"Yeah, that sounds pretty good." With a smile, he tossed the washcloth into the bathroom, heading to the dresser. Digging through, he found her a pair of shorts with a draw-string. "Max?"

"Yeah, babe?"

"Do you have any more of those SWAT T-shirts?" He grinned, opening another drawer, pulling one of the black workout shirts out of it.

"Got one just for you," he said, tossing her the shirt. When she had dressed and bounded off in search of dessert, he stripped the bed, remaking it with fresh sheets. Ignoring their clothes thrown on the floor, he had just enough time to straighten the bed before she walked back into the room carrying two giant mugs.

"I found the stuff for floats," Karlie said, holding them up like an offering. Setting them on his dresser, he propped some pillows up against the headboard before climbing into bed wearing a fresh pair of flannel pants. Patting the bed between his legs, he waited until Karlie had settled against his chest before handing her the float.

Deciding on bingeing a season of *American Horror Story*, her choice not his, Max worked at eating his own float while not getting any in Karlie's hair. The ice cream had done the trick. He made a mental note for future reference as she snuggled against him, turning her head against his chest every time the show became too scary.

This was the life he wanted, this was what he was willing to walk through fire every day for. It was nothing more than Karlie curled in his arms, laughing every time she had to hide her face while two mostly finished mugs of ice cream melted on the dresser next to them. But it was perfect.

CHAPTER
Fourteen

KARLIE HAD BEEN dead asleep when something woke her the next morning. Prying an eye open, she tried to figure out where she was. Feeling the hard body move underneath her, she remembered not just where she was but why she didn't have any clothes on.

After falling asleep in the middle of being half scared out of her mind, she had woken up really wanting to put some of her Google research to the test. She had still been too sore for more sex, but Max hadn't seemed to mind her refining her blow job skills on him. They must have been pretty decent since he had immediately ripped her clothes back off and made her ride his face while he ate her like a man who had been starving.

Just the thought of what they had done last night made her body heat up. She couldn't believe she had basically asked him for sex, then freaked out when he tried to do what she asked. Why Max had decided he wanted to be with her, she didn't think she would ever understand. But none of that answered the question of what had woken her up.

"Chi, get out of my room." Oh, that answered the question.

"Oh my god, Max. I am so sorry."

"Get. Out," Max repeated as he slung one of his pillows at his sister standing in the door of his bedroom with her hand over her mouth. Reaching down, he pulled the covers up, hiding most of their bodies from his stunned sister. Turning quickly, she hurried out of the room.

"Fuck, that's what I get for letting them have a key." Karlie started to giggle. She couldn't help it. It figured that the first time she had sex with a man she got caught, by his sister no less. "It's not funny," Max growled out. She tried to stop, but it was impossible and soon they were both laughing.

"And you told me you didn't have sex in public," Karlie said, smacking him lightly on the chest. Before she knew it, she was pinned underneath him.

"I guess it could have been worse. She could have gotten a lovely view of my ass while I was pounding into you, as you so eloquently put it last night." Karlie laughed again, drawing a smile from Max. She watched as his face suddenly sobered above her.

"Thank you," he said quietly.

"For what?" She couldn't imagine what she had done to merit his gratitude. She reached up, laying her hand against his cheek, loving the way his rough stubble felt against her hand. Her core immediately clenched, remembering how it had felt against her inner thighs.

Turning his head, he kissed her palm before his eyes returned to hers. He was so beautiful with his dark eyes, tanned skin and messy hair sticking out at crazy angles.

"For last night. For giving me your virginity. For trusting me not to hurt you more than I had to." Max leaned down, placing a gentle kiss to the corner of her mouth.

When he started to pull away, Karlie wrapped her arms around his neck, pulling him back down for a deeper one. As it turned to something more carnal, she winced when he rolled his hips against her. She must have made a noise because he instantly stopped rising to his knees.

"I'm sorry," Karlie whispered. She felt so stupid. This would all be so much easier if she had just done this in high school. But then, she wouldn't have shared it with Max and that seemed almost criminal.

"Baby, I can see your gears cranking from here." Maybe she could think up some stupid awkward thought to distract him. At the very least, she could throw out something about nipple rings.

"You know, I really hate to admit this," her eyes snapped up to his, finding a grin lighting up his face. Was that a tinge of pink she also saw on his skin? "But, I kind of like the idea of you walking around sore."

"Like an ego boost?"

"Pretty much. Come on, let's get breakfast. I have to spend most of the day studying for my procedure test. Sunday, I have to spend part of the day at the range."

Sliding off the bed, Max pulled on a pair of sweats that hung on his hips perfectly. Karlie quickly grabbed the shorts and SWAT T-shirt that had landed on her side of the bed, following him to the kitchen.

"Hey, at least we got breakfast out of my sister's breaking and entering this morning." Max turned to show her a plate of puffy donuts. "Bomboloni," he announced, making Karlie study them closer. "Here, they're like cream-filled donuts."

Taking a bite, she moaned as the sweet cream exploded in her mouth. How can anything that looked so ordinary taste so good?

"God, these are amazing," she said through bites.

"Yeah, Mom always made them to cheer us kids up if we were struggling." He took a big bite, chewing thoughtfully. "I would guess by now, she probably knows she wasted her time." Karlie snorted a laugh, blowing tiny bits of donut across the bar she was sitting at.

"Please tell me your sister won't tell your mom she caught us in bed this morning."

"Oh, she definitely will. I'm just amazed she hasn't dragged me to confession yet."

"I can't ever face your mother again," Karlie announced, turning pink.

"That's going to be a long life of avoiding someone who lives less than a block away. She might as well get used to it now. I'm not stopping pounding into you."

She gave Max her best stink eye, which just made him laugh. How was she supposed to know the stories she had heard in high school weren't quite accurate?

After breakfast, they had showered separately at Max's insistence, citing he couldn't be responsible for his actions otherwise. Settling onto his couch with his laptop open on her lap, Karlie worked on a group project due after Thanksgiving. Max spread his binders out on the small table, sliding in his earbuds.

It was almost lunch before Karlie noticed her stomach growling. She had made good progress on her portion of the project. Closing the laptop, she turned to see if Max was hungry, yet finding him watching her, his knee bobbing up and down under the table.

"What are you doing?" she asked when he pulled the earbuds from his ears.

"I was thinking about doing you," he replied with a smirk. Even his smirks were sexy.

"Will you finish your story?"

"Nope, you'll just have to be surprised." She watched him close the notebook, straightening his notes in a neat stack.

"Well, how about if you decide the table isn't too far away? You could pick up the story from there. Speaking of the table, did you know a single bacterium on it can multiply into around a billion in ten hours?" Max laughed, shaking his head.

"So you want to add to that by having sex against it?"

"Against it? I thought we would be on it." Max laughed again, standing up.

"I'm not sure it's that sturdy, besides I can pound better if you're just holding on to it." Karlie set the laptop on the coffee table. Standing up on the couch so she would be his height, she gave Max her best glare.

"Now you're just being a jerk," she said.

His resulting grin made her even more irritated. Setting his manuals on the counter in the kitchen, Max walked over to the couch. Wrapping a strong arm around her, he swung her off the couch into his arms.

"What are you doing?" Karlie asked with a squeal.

"I was going to show you what table sex is," he said. Karlie bit her bottom lip in anticipation. That was no small nightstick he was sporting. "What?" he growled. She slapped a hand over her mouth to prevent a giggle from escaping.

"Nothing, officer. I just locked my key inside. I'll do anything if you'll help me get it out." She batted her eyes at him with a smile as she watched his eyes grow impossibly dark with lust.

Looking around, he grabbed his handcuffs out of his utility belt. Karlie gasped when he set her on her feet, shoving her down against the table as he held her in place with his hips.

"Ma'am, I'm going to need to frisk this hot, tight body first. Are you going to be good for me or bad?" Karlie responded by rocking her hips against him. She grinned when she heard him growl. Faster than she knew possible, he had her hands in restraints behind her back.

"Tell me if they're too tight," he whispered before taking a step back, holding her in place with one hand. "Do you know it's a crime to hide this fine of an ass away inside a pair of sweatpants that are obviously three times too large?"

She gasped when she felt his hands ease inside the waistband of the sweats she had pulled on after her shower. Karlie had assumed his version of table sex would be fast and hard, but Max worked the pants off at an agonizingly slow pace. Hearing him kneel on the floor behind her, he held her steady as he helped her step out of them.

Heat seared her when he placed a hand on her hip, wrapping long fingers around it to hold her in place as he laid kisses on her backside.

"Do you know it took everything I had not to touch this ass that night? I could almost see it under your shorts." Karlie jumped when she felt his hand come down on her ass with an audible smack.

The heat building in her core only doubled when he followed the sting by running his tongue over it. This was a far cry from what she had been led to believe. She only had a moment to clench her thighs together before Max kicked her legs open.

"Max," she moaned when she felt him press his erection into her ass again.

"These cuffs are going to get in the way," he answered, unhooking them to move her hands above her before cuffing the heavy metal around her wrist again. Now she lay with her upper body spread across the table, her ass in the air as he stood behind her.

A condom dropped onto the table next to her head. She couldn't control her hips from grinding against him this time, her body already knowing what it craved.

"Dirty little coed got me hard with her eye fucking when she opened the door, her pert round tits on display under that tank." Wrapping his arm around her, he slid his fingers through her folds. "Fuck, you're so wet. Does this turn my dirty girl on?"

She answered him with a moan when he slid a finger into her as he thrust gently against her ass. Rocking against his hand, she knew he was turning her into something animalistic, but she needed to chase the feeling building in her body.

She barely registered the tear of foil before he was in her. The low scream that came out of her mouth was more from the surprise of being filled completely than from pain this time. He didn't give her time to adjust before he was pounding into her from behind.

Struggling to keep her toes on the floor as he rocked the table under her, she felt the wave build as she began to chant his name. When her climax finally slammed into her, she lost track of Max. It was impossible to know where he ended and she began, he filled all of her senses so completely.

"Are you okay, baby?" Max was still pressed up against her, placing gentle kisses on her shoulder. Stretching over her, he unlocked the handcuffs, tossing them on the table.

"Max."

"I know, I'm pulling out. Hold on." She heard a hiss behind her as he stepped away. It felt like a loss somehow. Great, less than twenty-four hours of sex, and she was already addicted to his cock.

"You're addicted, huh?" Seriously, why did she insist on saying everything out loud? "Good, then my fiendish plan is working," he added. Laughing, she stood up, stretching her back. She was going to pick up the pace in the gym if sex with Max continued at this pace.

"So was that the fantasy you had in mind?" she asked.

Max looked up at her from where he had kneeled to help her back into the sweats. Wow, he just thought she had eye fucked him before. The condom had disappeared, but he hadn't bothered to button his pants back up. Those romance novel covers had nothing on the man kneeling in front of her.

"Babe, that was so much better than anything I've been jacking off to. By the way, that was pounding."

"Oh my god, Max." She laughed, stopping midstep into the sweats.

"What? What do you think has been sustaining me the last four months?" Working her pants up her legs, he raised the T-shirt to kiss her stomach when they were in place.

As he stood, she wrapped her arms around his neck, pulling him to her for a kiss. Karlie felt her heart skip when Max picked her up in his arms to walk to the couch. Snuggling into his chest when he sat down, she ran a hand up to cradle his cheek.

"Did you know it only takes four minutes to know if you like someone?" she asked. Max snuggled her against him tighter.

"Is that so?"

"Did you know that falling in love has the same neurological effects as snorting cocaine?"

"I can see that. I've seen the effects of cocaine."

"Did you know that expressing gratitude for someone you love causes an immediate spike to your happiness?"

Max turned her loose, pulling her around until she was straddling his lap.

"In that case, I'm grateful that I was on call the night you locked your key in the apartment. I'm doubly grateful that I kept chasing that high that led me to you over and over. And I am really fucking grateful that someone told me to get my head out of my ass and go get you back."

Karlie grinned at him. "Well, I'm grateful that you looked like a wet dream in your uniform so I couldn't stay away after those first four minutes. And, don't get mad, but I'm glad I needed to kiss you so bad that I blew up the entire campus so you had to fight to keep us together."

Max laughed, pulling her in for another kiss. She could already feel his erection under her ass growing.

"Really, again?" she asked, pulling back.

"I can't help it, it knows where it belongs." With a feigned sigh, she collapsed against his chest.

"Max."

"Yeah, babe."

"Thank you for making this the best school year ever." Lifting her up into a sitting position, he laid his forehead against hers.

"Baby, we haven't even gotten started yet."

Epilogue

"ARE you sure you want to take me?" Max asked, pulling on his T-shirt in the bedroom. Karlie was brushing her teeth in the bathroom. Ignoring him until she was done, she leaned against the doorjamb, watching as he slid on his boots.

"Of course I'm taking you. It's snowing outside, you can't ride your bike. We're expecting three feet by tonight."

Standing, he pulled her to him, placing a sloppy kiss on her lips. Life had become a perfect mix of crazy in the month they had officially been together.

He had insisted that both Karlie and Sam join his family for Thanksgiving, since neither one could go home. Karlie had spent half of the day before cooking with his mom and sister. They had all had a hilarious time together, getting into the wine a little too much.

Fortunately, either Chiara had never mentioned walking in on them in bed or his mother pretended she didn't know anything about it.

"I don't think I'll be done until late," he said.

"Don't worry about me. I have two finals today, then Sam and I are going to hang before she heads out tomorrow."

Max blew out a breath with a scowl. He didn't like the

idea of her driving in the snow. First, she was from Texas and her snow driving abilities were terrifying at best. Second, well, he really didn't have anything else except she really was scary.

"The four-wheel-drive works and I'll drive slow," she said with an exasperated sigh, reading his mind. Winter had come early this year, after all, with it dumping snow starting right after Thanksgiving.

"Come on, you're going to be late." Finished dressing, he followed her to the door of his apartment, shrugging on his coat.

Hanging on to him as they climbed down the stairs to her truck, he managed to keep Karlie upright. He got a kick out of watching her walk across the snowy driveway like it was a skating rink. She had explained to him that the part of Texas she was from usually just got ice storms. After settling her into the passenger side of her truck, he backed out of his driveway.

"Are you nervous?" she asked when he had merged into traffic on the way across town.

"Not really. I'll either make it or not. It really comes down to training in the end." Today was the day he took his final test to become a SWAT officer. He would know by the end of shift today what his fate would be.

"That's good. I think I'm nervous enough for both of us." He grinned as she laced her fingers through his. Lifting her hand to his mouth, he kissed her knuckles softly.

"You have your marketing and law finals today?" he asked. They drove the rest of the way to police headquarters as she told him every detail of what her finals entailed.

Pulling up out front, he put the truck in park before climbing out. When she was in the driver's seat, he pulled her to him for one more kiss.

"My god, I rambled the whole way here, didn't I? Why didn't you stop me?" Max kissed her again. "I love you, Max.

You're going to do great," she whispered when he stepped back.

"How could I not with you cheering me on?" Closing her door, he waved as she pulled back out into traffic. Lifting his face to the sky, he said a silent prayer she made it without racking up any property damage.

Walking into the SWAT office, he was greeted by Troy with a schedule of today's testing.

"Report to the doc for a physical first. He'll release you for today, as well as make you pee in a cup. When you're done, report for psych testing. Good luck."

Max walked to the office the doctor used when he had physicals to perform for evaluations. Stripping to his boxer briefs, Max went through a routine of motions to prove he could handle the stress the job would have on his body. His vision was perfect, as were his hearing and heart. His thigh had healed and he had no hernias.

After giving a urine sample, he redressed, heading over to the Psychologist.

"So, Max, tell me about what led to you receiving a reprimand for sexual harassment?" the woman started as soon as he had filled out all of the paperwork. He knew she was testing his reaction to the one subject that had the ability to immediately piss him off.

Taking a deep breath, he reminded himself to stay calm as he succinctly walked her through what had happened on campus. There seemed to be no subject concerning him that was off-limits. He had his integrity questioned, his ability to reason pushed to the limit and even his past gang task force performance reviewed.

Finally, with a serious nod, he was dismissed.

"How did that go?" Troy asked him when he returned to find him in the office.

"I have no idea."

"Yeah, feels like you got a prostate exam twice, right?"

"At least twice."

Troy chuckled before checking his schedule. "Okay, get suited up in full tactical. We'll start with the run, move to the obstacle course, then do a recovery run."

With a nod, Max headed to the equipment room to pull on his tactical gear. He was tying his boots when Troy stuck his head into the room.

"You don't need a gas mask but bring both sets of glasses." Max nodded, pulling his vest on full of gear he might need in the field. After Troy inspected him to make sure there wasn't anything else necessary, Max followed him outside. The rest of the team was standing on the side of the building when they got there.

"Okay, Max. You're going to run the same route you've been training on as fast as you can. Here's a weapon," he said, handing him one of the assault rifles. "You won't need your helmet for this."

When Max was ready, the team counted down until he took off. It was no easy thing to run in so much gear in the snow, but he only had to make it a half mile in six minutes. When he reached the quarter mile mark, he turned, heading back.

As he approached the end puffing, he could hear the rest of the team cheering him on. Crossing the finish, he only had a second to catch his breath before Troy was screaming at him to get his ass to the obstacle course. The rest of the team followed as he jogged across the street.

There were members of one of the other teams placed around the course as he started to work his way through in full gear, including his helmet. He crawled for thirty yards on his belly with the rifle, he scaled a six-foot fence, he did push-ups, pull-ups and sit-ups all in his gear.

He was pretty sure the hardest part of the test was pulling a tank of a man twenty yards safely, both wearing full gear. That was, until he had to heave Davis onto his back and run the stairs to the fourth floor of headquarters, then bring him back down. Setting him carefully back on the ground, after hearing a myriad of threats about dropping him the entire time, Max debated throwing up. Either that or passing out, whichever.

"Let's get your gear off for lunch. We'll head to the range next." Max nodded weakly before being pulled off the ground where he had kneeled to set Davis down.

"Come on, man. You're doing great." Troy led the team across the street to a deli on the corner where he bought Max's food.

"When does the girlfriend head home for Christmas?" Troy asked, sitting down next to him.

"Day after tomorrow. She has one more final that morning." They shot the bull as they ate. Much to Max's relief, they took their time enjoying their lunch. He really didn't want to see it again somewhere during his testing.

When they were done, they headed back to the range. Max had been introduced to a wide range of weapons that most cops didn't handle. He easily passed the handgun round, moving on to assault rifles before finishing with correctly identifying the other weapons, their uses and operation.

After completing a stress shooting course where he had to memorize a picture of an assailant then pick him out of the different innocents that popped up, Troy had him get geared back up for his last test. It would be a situation that he had to not only figure out how to solve, but keep his team from getting hurt. When he was ready, they drove to an abandoned building that they had trained in weeks ago.

"Okay, Max. The situation is there are several hostages being held in a back room. We need to breach the building safely, secure the hostages and take out the perpetrators. You'll have to find a safe point of entry, work your way through the building to let your team in, then finish the mission."

Max looked up at the building as they climbed out of the vehicle. He had been given schematics on the way here that he had studied. Looking at the first floor, he saw no way in that wasn't secured.

"There should be a fire escape to the roof on the outside of the building. I can lower into one of those boarded-up windows on the third floor," Max said, pulling the rappelling gear out of the back.

Attaching his communications earpiece, he ran a check before starting toward the building. The rest of the team would spread out around the exterior to wait for further information from him. Finding the old fire escape, Max prayed it would hold his weight to the top.

Reaching the top of the building, he quickly hooked up his ropes after checking in. He had spied an opening with a metal grate screwed to the wall on his way up, not far from his position. It had holes in the grate which would allow him to look inside with the camera he had brought.

Securing his line to the roof, he eased over the side of the building, offering up his second prayer of the day as he descended to the opening. Setting the brake on his ropes, he pulled the small camera out of his pocket. Inserting it into one of the holes, he studied the screen until he was positive there was no activity inside.

Studying the grate, he gave himself a small pat on the back for thinking to include a small handheld automatic drill in his pockets. Spraying each screw with a blast from a tiny can of loosener, he used the drill to back the screws out. Catching the grate in his hand, he leaned in the window, placing it quietly on the floor.

Sliding inside, he carefully unhooked his lines listening for any activity. Radioing his team, he proceeded toward the doorway, careful to walk as silently as possible. He knew there were stairs at both ends of the building, so he turned left, heading down the hallway.

Almost making it to the second floor, he had to duck into one of the rooms when he heard footsteps on the stairs below him. Watching from the darkness as a man walked past him, Max shadowed him until he entered one of the rooms.

Using his small camera, Max counted four guys sitting at a table playing cards as two others, one man and one woman, sat tied in chairs in the corner. Max was pretty sure he knew at least three of them from patrol, but it didn't matter.

Careful not to make any noise, he marked the location of their position before continuing back to the stairwell. Reaching the bottom floor, he checked his compass for his location before radioing his team. He knew they would get in position to enter the building as soon as he could make an opening.

Bending down, he accessed the nearest doorway leading outside. A large piece of tin had been screwed into the wall to block access. Using his drill again, he backed as many screws out as possible before peeling the tin back, letting the team in.

With the information he had collected, Troy helped him lay out the best plan for extraction of the hostages. Two of the team headed across the building to come from the back while the remaining four returned up the stairs he had just come down.

When they were in position, Max held his hand up, counting down the seconds on his fingers. As his fist closed, he tossed a flash-bang grenade in the room, following it through the door. Racing to secure one of the perpetrators, he ducked when the man swung at him.

Within a matter of seconds, all four men were on the ground with their hands cuffed in zip ties behind them. They were walked down the stairs as they followed two of his team members helping the hostages. Reaching the bottom, they worked their way past the tin until everyone was outside.

Flicking his knife open, Max released all of the men that had helped with the exercise.

"Shit, Troy. Did your new guy have to blind us all?" one of the guys grumbled.

"Maybe next time, you should pay attention," Troy responded teasingly with a slap to the guy's back.

"I got to say, though, that might be one of the fastest times yet," another one said.

"Not too bad. Let's head back to HQ." Troy led the team toward their police van.

"Hey, your kid owes us a beer this weekend," the man Max had thrown on the ground said.

"Don't worry. He'll pay up. I'll let you know where." Troy climbed into the driver's side after storing his gear in the back. "Hope you're good for it, Max. Those guys drink like fish."

"I'm good for it. I'll call the guy at Donnelly's for a table Friday." Max laid his head on the back of the seat. He was exhausted, but it was a good exhausted. If asked, he could honestly say he had done his best.

Parking the van, Troy left the team standing in the hall as he walked into the commander's office. Looking out the windows, Max watched the snow increase as he waited for his fate to be determined. Nothing about this experience had been normal protocol, including this. He could do nothing but wait, but at least the rest of the team waited with him.

"Scaletti." His heart raced when he heard the commander call his name as he stepped out of his office.

"Sir," he said, coming to attention. The commander looked him over once before sticking out his hand.

"Welcome to SWAT." The other team members slapped him on the back as he felt a stupid grin break out on his face.

"Thank you, sir," he answered, shaking his hand.

"Hey, Scaletti." Turning when he heard his former commanding officer call his name at the end of the hall, he tried to make sense out of what he was seeing.

"I found these frozen in the snow outside waiting for

you."

"Karlie?" he asked as she stepped toward him. She looked at him with the most hopeful expression he had ever seen on someone's face.

"Max?" she asked, standing in the hall. When he smiled at her, she broke into a run, slamming into him. This time, though, when she crashed into him instead of a gym wall, he felt several hands on his back to steady him. With both arms wrapped around his neck, she kissed him with everything she had.

"I guess now I see what all the fuss was about." The other men started laughing at Commander Taylor's words, turning Karlie's face red when she pulled back. Soon Karlie's friends, including Chiara, surrounded them cheering.

"I'm so proud of you. I love you," Karlie said before lowering herself back to the ground.

"I love you too," he answered, holding her in his arms.

"Sir, I would like to volunteer for campus duty," Davis said, making everyone laugh.

Max looked down at Karlie. He had taken everything he thought he needed in life and had thrown it away the second she had opened the front door of that apartment. Without a second thought, he knew he would go through it all again, being shot by a gang leader, assigned a campus job, getting fired for an innocent kiss if it meant he would wind up right where he was at this moment.

"What do you say we go celebrate, then go home?" Max said to Karlie when she turned her face up to him.

"Sounds perfect. I'd like to explore what's been hiding under all that Kevlar. Did you know SWAT officers are ranked above campus cops on the hotness scale?"

"I'm not sure that scale exists," Max said, raising an eyebrow at her.

"Max! The internet doesn't lie." He grinned as Karlie took his hand.

Fact or Fiction

Or

Things That Make You Go Hmmm

One of the best parts of reading a scientifically inspired action/adventure book is the section in the back that explains what in the story was fact and what was fiction. Now I know what you're thinking, dear reader, how could anything in this book be fact?

That's exactly what I think when I'm lying in bed at night after reading the back of a James Rollins novel. No one told me we could all be wiped out by nanobots or something else equally nefarious. Thanks for the insomnia, Mr. Rollins! Anyway, without further ado, enjoy.

THE HOUSE - FACT

Yes, somewhere in New England is a large gray and atomic orange house. Yes, it did house students, but not anymore. The original second floor included five bedrooms with eight women and one very small bathroom. If you were assigned to one of the rooms on the stairway landing, it required three keys to access everywhere (one for the room, one for the front door, and one for the living areas.)

THE CAMPUS POLICE - FACT WITH A LOT OF FICTION

The police on this campus are extremely professional. There was not even a rumor of one taking up with a student, but then they didn't look like Max. Most campus police officers are experienced (older) with a significant amount of hours of extra training just to qualify to be on campus.

They do open doors if you lock yourself out without making you feel like an idiot. They also made sure the kids with practice that didn't finish until after sundown made it home safely. I can also assure you that the overall police force in this town is one of the best looking I've ever seen. Please, I'm begging you, put out a calendar!

THE STOVE FROM HELL - FACT

So there wasn't an awesome fireball, but mice had eaten all of the insulation and it did smoke out the apartment. The outside of the stove would heat up to match the inside. The thermostat had broken long before, so it was a crapshoot how hot to cook something or how long.

One of the burners would shock you if you touched a metal spoon to the pan while heating something. It was a good lesson on using wooden spoons. It was "repaired" after it caught on fire.

THE BUFFALO BILL BASEMENT - FACT

Creepiest ass basement ever! I swear every time anyone went down the steps, you could hear an audience yelling not to go. There was one washer and dryer for the house shared by twenty-two people. No one ever figured out what was in the padlocked closet. I vote Hannibal Lecter or Leatherface. Maybe that clown from *IT*. Definitely at least one chupacabra.

THE CAMPUS MEDICAL CENTER - FACT

Most colleges really are convinced the campus is ground zero for STDs. Sprained ankle? Must be an STD. Concussion? STD. Sore throat? STD. Okay, that last one could be legitimate.

THE SQUIRRELS - FACT

Definition: Fluffy balls of demonic cuteness put on this earth to lull us into a false sense of friendly adorableness. Mine have managed to eat the stuffing out of every cushion on my front porch.

The campus ones were huge and either threw your trash back at you or popped out themselves while you were tossing your trash. They would also steal food out from under you if you didn't watch.

———

I hope you enjoyed book one in the New England Romance series. Pick up book two, *Best Laid Schemes*, coming in September 2022, for more "that can't be right" moments in the continuing saga of the campus apartment. Cheers!

Don't miss *Combustible*, the newest book in The Inhuman Protectors Romance Series releasing July 2022.

If you've enjoyed *Nothing Ventured*, please leave a review on your favorite book sites.

For all things Avery Samson, sign up for the newsletter:
www.averysamsonbooks.newletter

Did you know I have a reader group? Join Avery Samson's
Unicorn Readers here:
Unicorn Readers

Also by Avery Samson

Acknowledgments

I've have the amazingly good fortune to be surrounded by a great team. No matter how much I thank them, I can never do justice to how much they continue to help me along this journey.

Thank you to the following for their invaluable work:

Ellie at My Brother's Editor for catching my many, many grammatical errors. We've been together for two years, here's to many more.

Heather and her team at Elle Woods PR who makes sure my hard work gets noticed.

Jackie for doing, well, whatever I ask of her. Including helping keep me from going insane when I have too many balls in the air.

Rachel with RH Creative Designs for everything. Not only does she take a random picture of a man's torso and turn it into something magical, but also manages to find time for everything else I need. And, for the record, she is the expert on all things volleyball.

My family and friends for sharing their college horror stories. Some where mine, but many were their stories. Did the apartment on the second floor exist? Definitely. Was living there as dramatic as in the book? Not really. Do we still laugh about the horrors experienced there? Absolutely.

Finally, thank you to everyone who blogged, ARC read, promoted, and chose *Nothing Ventured* to be their next read. You will forever hold a special place in my heart.

About the Author

Avery Samson grew up on a ranch outside of a small west Texas town. Since she could remember, she's had her face stuck in a book. She left ranch life after high school for the big city of Fort Worth.

After living all over the state of Texas, she now finds herself back on one of the family ranches near Dallas with her husband surrounded by cattle. A lot of them. They're everywhere! When not traveling or reading, she spends her time writing.

Avery would love for you to follow her. She's everywhere (just like those damn cows.)

Join my newsletter for all the latest news.
averysamsonbooks.com/newsletter

Visit my website for my current book list.
averysamsonbooks.com

Join my reader group.
https://bit.ly/30fZ7N8

Like me on Facebook.
https://www.facebook.com/averysamsonauthor

Follow me on Instagram.

https://www.instagram.com/averysamson91/

Check out my Pinterest page.
https://www.pinterest.com/averysamson91/

9 798201 776466